FRIEND IS NOT A VERB

FRIEND IS NOT A VERB

A NOVEL BY

DANIEL EHRENHAFT

An Imprint of HarperCollinsPublishers

For Nathaniel Benjamin Ehrenhaft:
Welcome to the wacky human race!

HarperTeen is an imprint of HarperCollins Publishers.

Friend Is Not a Verb
www.harperteen.com

Library of Congress Cataloging-in-Publication Data
Ehrenhaft, Daniel.
     Friend is not a verb : a novel / by Daniel Ehrenhaft. — 1st ed.
         p.   cm.
     Summary: While sixteen-year-old Hen's family and friends try to make his supposed
dreams of becoming a rock star come true, he deals with the reality of being in a band
with an ex-girlfriend, a friendship that may become love, and his older sister's mysterious
disappearance and reappearance.
     ISBN 978-0-06-113106-6
     [1. Interpersonal relations—Fiction. 2. Bands (Music)—Fiction. 3. Brothers
and sisters—Fiction. 4. Fugitives from justice—Fiction. 5. Family life—New York
(State)—New York—Fiction. 6. New York (N.Y.)—Fiction.] I. Title.
PZ7.E3235Fri 2010   2009044006
[Fic]—dc22   CIP
                                                                              AC

Typography by Thomas Forget
        10 11 12 13 14 LP/RRDB 10 9 8 7 6 5 4 3 2 1
                            ❖
                        First Edition

The year was marked by ominous signs: fires blazed in the sky, there was a violent earthquake, and a cow talked. There was a rumor that a cow had talked the previous year, but nobody believed it. This year, they did.

—*Roman historian Titus Livius (59 BCE–17 CE), The Early History of Rome*

When the going gets weird, the weird turn pro.

—*Hunter S. Thompson*

Acknowledgments

Parts of this book have been fifteen years in the making (gulp) so it's only fair to give thanks to the writing group where I first began throwing out ideas. So here's to Jill Hoffman, Jennifer Belle, Scott Jones, and everyone else who met on Franklin Street all those years ago. Thanks are also due to Joanna Hershon, Merrill Feitell, Bowman Hastie, and Barney Miller (I'm sure I'm forgetting people) who read parts of this book in various forms along the way. Enormous gratitude is owed to my agents, Edward Necarsulmer IV and Sarah Burnes. Ditto the good folks at Harper for brilliant editorial advice, above all Clare Hutton, Gretchen Hirsch, and Zareen Jaffery. Farrin Jacobs and Elise Howard deserve a shout, too. So do Maureen Johnson, Rachel Cohn, and E. Lockhart—you rule! And the biggest thanks, as always, to my insanely patient and ingenious spouse, Jessica.

Opening Disclaimers

This is kind of a screwy story, so I'm not sure where to begin. I mean, I could tell you my name, but I've decided to change it. Seriously. I don't know what the new one will be yet, but as soon as I figure it out, I'm going to file the forms and petition the court and do whatever it takes to make it official—and if it costs money, then I'll finally get a real job. Or at least I'll play the Lotto.

Until I hit the jackpot, though, I'm stuck with Henry Birnbaum. Hen, for short.

Everyone has always called me Hen. All the major players in this screwy story have: my big sister, Sarah (who vanished under mysterious circumstances for an entire year); my girlfriend, Petra (who dumped me); my best friend, Emma (who also had that dream about going to school naked); my parents (who threatened to set fire to my dirty socks unless I "took responsibility for [my] own hygiene and put them in the hamper!"); and, lastly, Gabriel Stern, my sister's friend from college, the twenty-two-year-old fugitive who was supposed to be my bass teacher but ended up being something else entirely (a bizarro Obi-Wan to my Luke? I'm still trying to figure it out), partly because he is such a lousy bassist himself.

The problem is, Hen doesn't fit me anymore. It's too young sounding. True, I am only sixteen, but after all the insanity of the past year, sometimes I feel like I'm a hundred. Sometimes I feel like I'm a thousand. Or that I've moved beyond life and death, like I'm a mummy with ancient mystical wisdom locked up inside my sarcophagus, just waiting to be unleashed. Not that I look particularly wise or ancient or mystical. Frizzy brown mop top plus pale broomstick body doesn't exactly add up to Father Time. I don't know what it adds up to. Time to score a fake ID?

Anyway, my new name, whatever it is, will say something about me. Like "the guy who finally learned the freakish truth about *why* his sister disappeared." Or "He may be going through that awkward teen phase now, but watch out soon, ladies!" Except it won't be that long. It'll be short and tasty, like a choice bass line (think funky, like Bootsy Collins)—maybe in one of those forgotten tribal languages Gabriel tried to learn while he and my sister were hiding out in the Caribbean. Those indigenous Caribbean tribes know how to do names right. (In Taino, the name "Yaya" means "the Great Spirit who Created Everything." I would say that's funky. At the very least, it's funkier

x

than Henry Birnbaum, which means absolutely nothing.)

Most of all, my new name will show how I've become more superstitious. How I no longer believe that there's any difference between what happens while you're asleep and while you're awake—aside from the obvious stuff, like snoring and drooling. Or how if you turn your dream life and real life inside out, you'll wind up in the same place: the scary, buck-ass-naked place where everything is right in the open for you to see, even if you don't want to.

Which I think is what Gabriel wanted me to believe. Not that he said it in those words. He said, "Hen, the way I see it, a person's subconscious is like a port-o-john. It's dark and nasty, right? If it could smell, it would smell like a thousand butts. But sometimes nature calls. Sometimes you gotta go in there. So here's my advice to you: The next time you absolutely have to take care of business in a real port-o-john, like at an outdoor concert or something, first take a minute to stand inside it— even if there's a line waiting. Just close your eyes and breathe in the stink. Because you know what'll happen? Pretty soon you won't even *notice* the stink anymore. I swear. And then when you're all done and you step outside, the open air will be a brand-new thing. It'll be the most beautiful thing you've ever smelled. You'll want to hug all those impatient people in line. Get it?"

That's a direct quote, by the way. I recorded it.

Right now, I just want to state for the record: I know that this preamble might not make a whole lot of sense. Or it may just sound gross. Or worse, it may sound corny, like a preview for a pretentious big-budget movie—you know, with an opening camera shot that would pan over our house in Brooklyn and a thunderous voiceover, *"In a Troubled Time . . . in an Age of Upheaval . . . secrets will be revealed about Henry Birnbaum and his sister, Sarah, and her friend Gabriel . . ."* like there should be violins blasting as you read this. But it's true. Everything I'm about to tell you actually did happen.

So enough with the opening disclaimers. If I'm going to throw open the symbolic port-o-john door, there really is only one place to start. That would be June 4, the first night of summer vacation. That was the night Petra decided she didn't want to be my girlfriend anymore—back when my sister was still missing, back when I still hated Gabriel Stern's guts . . . back when I blamed Gabriel and my sister for almost everything that had gone wrong in my life, even though I hardly knew him or why he and Sarah had disappeared in the first place.

PART I

The Two Days Leading Up to the Conclusion That
Becoming a Rock Star Would Solve All My Problems

CHAPTER ONE

Feelings

"I'm sorry, Hen. I still have feelings for you. It's just that my band needs a real bass player now. We're not a joke band anymore. Okay, sweetie?"

That was how Petra Dostoyevsky fired me.

We were standing outside the Bimbo Lounge on the Lower East Side of Manhattan. It was raining: heavy, pelting rain. Cars were honking; pedestrians were irritable; Petra's hair dye was starting to run. The black drops on her cheeks were actually kind of attractive, which annoyed me. It was 9:05 P.M. Her favorite band—aside from her own—was supposed to start at 9:00. (They're called Shakes the Clown. Petra believes that they're geniuses. According to her, they're the "new Flaming Lips.")

"We should still hang out," Petra added, peeking at her watch.

I nodded. I couldn't imagine any possible scenario where that might occur, but it was a nice thought.

She cast a furtive glance at the bouncer. He was bald and pale, about the size and shape of a rhinoceros. He wore a tight 2002 Britney Spears concert T-shirt under a soggy pin-striped blazer, with a Steal Your Parents' Money pin on the lapel.

"Do you still want to see the show?" she asked.

"Um, no, I guess not. But—"

"Bye, Hen." She pecked me on the cheek, then turned and scurried past the bouncer—who not only held the door, but also graciously neglected to card her.

I prefer the word "fired" to "dumped," because going out with Petra was kind of like a job. Not that I'm ungrateful. Being with Petra—and being the bassist for her band, PETRA—was amazing for the month that it lasted. She was the first real girlfriend I'd ever had. But it was hard work. She's pretty much a superstar—at Franklin High, anyway—so the playing field was never level. She's tall (two inches taller than me), tasteful in regard to piercings (a lone silver stud in the left nostril); she's got a mixed pedigree, like Barack Obama (though she looks more white than black); and she even manages to pull off hair dye unpretentiously (jet black, but somehow not in a scary way).

Plus, I'm fairly sure she's smarter than I am.

So it was no surprise that she treated me the way a boss would. A nice boss, sure. "That's not how the bass line goes, sweetie." Or: "That T-shirt doesn't look cute on you, Hen; you should wear this ironic one." She even kissed me with bosslike detachment,

4

warmly and professionally. I don't want to get into the specifics, but let's just say that there were no spontaneous moments of wild passion. She operated on a reward system. If I nailed a bass line she wrote or wore the right T-shirt, I got lucky.

The funny thing is, I never would have gone out with her in the first place if I hadn't responded to her ad in the school's online paper, *The Franklin Sentinel*. It wasn't a personal ad, either. It was an ad seeking a bassist for her band. And I guess that's the point: It's hard not to think of a relationship as a job when you have to be interviewed and pass an audition. On the other hand, that does sound ungrateful, and it's probably not fair to her, because there are certain moments in your life when you fall in love with a semistranger, instantly and deliriously—without even an initial crush. For me, that moment was when I read that ad. It came at the end of Petra's blog, "Please Kill Me."

PLEASE KILL ME
By Petra Dostoyevsky

Day 5,882 of a life that never seems to end . . .
"It would be an unsound fancy and self-contradictory to expect that things which have never yet been done can be done except by means which have never yet been tried."
                                        —*Sir Francis Bacon*

Dearest Franklinites,
You'll notice a quote above this week's post. I have no idea

what the quote means. Is that why I got a D on my last philosophy quiz? Maybe. But perhaps it would be helpful for all of us if I told you what I know about the author himself.

Sir Francis Bacon was a 17th-century English nobleman who revolutionized science and philosophy, forever altering mankind's attitudes toward these mysterious disciplines. He accomplished this amazing feat simply by asserting that he was a lot smarter than everyone else. (Bacon was not a humble man.) He also asserted that animal furs produce their own heat, like an electric wok. "This is why fur keeps us warm," he once said. "You feel it? It's like a sauna up in here." (I'm paraphrasing.)

Out of supreme admiration for the wise assertions of Bacon, I decided to prove his theory of heat correct. I dug my grandma's moth-eaten mink out of the closet and huddled naked over it on the sidewalk outside my mom's apartment building, to see if I got warm. Regrettably, this experiment caused some consternation among my neighbors, and I spent last night shackled to a desk at the Eighty-first Precinct.

But what does this tell us of Bacon himself? Sadly, nothing. There isn't much any of us can say about Bacon for certain, not even my philosophy teacher, other than that he did not smell very nice. People rarely bathed or washed their clothes in the 17th century. Stick deodorant would not be invented for at least another three hundred years. To his credit, however, Bacon does happen to share his name with a food product I feel has been unjustly *criticized in recent times. I don't know about you, but I'm too young to care about greasy fat and cholesterol. Bacon also has protein and tastes darn good.*

I digress. The point of this post: I won't be allowed to blog for a while, owing to poor grades, lack of focus, and an "attitude problem." So I'm starting a band. Why? Well I read somewhere once that "It would be unsound fancy and self-contradictory to think that things which have never yet been done can be done except by means which have never yet been tried." Couldn't have said it better myself. I am trying by means which have never been tried, friends! I already have a drummer lined up, the wildly talented Bartholomew Savage of the Spencer School, and I am the guitarist/front woman/vixen. (There, I said it.) Now I need a bassist. Do any of you play bass? If so, please hit me back at: petrad@franklin.edu . . . Auditions start tomorrow at 3:30 at Sonic Rehearsal Studios!

xoxo Petra

As far as the audition went:

I was the only one who showed up. Nobody else had bothered, probably because they assumed Petra was joking. Petra made a joke of everything, which was partly what made her such a superstar. The majority of beautiful girls at our school had no sense of humor at all. (Around me, anyway.) I remembered asking George Monroe, the guy who sat next to me in Civics, if he planned to audition. He plays bass for the jazz band, and you can tell he shreds. He just laughed.

Sure enough, when I arrived at Sonic Rehearsal Studios after a perfunctory email exchange, I felt like the victim of a prank. The "Studios" consisted of a single room at the back of a bodega. It wasn't much bigger than a broom closet. It *smelled* like a broom closet, dank and musty. The walls were draped with grimy yellow foam, the kind used to pack eggs—I imagine for soundproofing.

Petra stood alone amid the decrepit amplifiers and drums in a black sweater, miniskirt, leggings, and boots, all of which matched her hair dye. She smirked at me.

"Hi," I said, nervously clutching my bass case.

"Thanks for coming. Hen, isn't it?" Her dark eyes brightened. "Wait! I know you. You're that guy whose sister disappeared, right?"

"Yup, that's me," I said. "The guy whose sister disappeared."

"Oh, my God—" She clasped a hand over her mouth. "Sorry, that was so rude."

"Don't worry about it."

"But it was rude, wasn't it?"

"Depends on how you look at it," I said.

She stared down at her boots, then blinked shyly at me. "Well, let me make it up to you," she said. "Play me a song. I promise I'll be more objective than usual."

I glanced around. "Shouldn't we wait for your drummer? You know . . ." I couldn't remember his name, only that it had a great ring.

"He's not coming," she said. "It's just you and me. He was sort of bummed out. I mean, since you're the only one who answered the ad."

"Oh," I said.

Looking back now, I realize that this conversation may have marked the high point of our relationship. I plugged in and plucked out four measures of Queen's "Another One Bites the Dust." (If I were a pianist, this would be like auditioning with "Chopsticks.") Petra applauded wildly after my pathetic performance, then jumped forward and kissed me on the lips—quickly and naturally, as if we'd known each other for years. Her arms lingered on my shoulders. She told me I was in the band. She asked me if I wanted to come over to her mom's apartment that weekend, to work on her "material." I said yes.

I'd never felt as wonderful, not even when we made out in her bedroom two days later and officially became a couple for the next month. For better or worse, that's the God's honest truth. During that one moment, in that stuffy windowless cell with the foam egg packaging, I was in paradise.

Back to the night she fired me:

"On second thought, I do want to see the show," I imagined telling her, seconds into my brand-new role as her ex-boyfriend. What if I'd pretended to be cheerfully clueless? *"You said we should still hang out, right? Let's go!"* That would have been funny. On the other hand, she probably wouldn't have appreciated the joke. *"Hen, let's not make this one of those awkward*

moments," she would have told me earnestly.

So, all right, one thing that did bug me about Petra: She was funnier in writing than she was in person. A lot of times, even in normal conversation, she sounded as if she were pitching a TV commercial to a bunch of ad execs. She insisted that every recent pop-culture phenomenon was nothing more than a recycled bit of something brilliant in the past.

I wasn't so sure. What about MySpace when it first came out? That was new. Or how about the Steal Your Parents' Money sticker campaign? In case you're not from New York City or you don't remember: The previous summer, hundreds of plain button-sized stickers made headlines when they mysteriously appeared in subway cars all over the city. Nobody knew who posted them or why, and nobody credible ever claimed responsibility, although they were attributed variously to college pranksters, aging hippies, and the MTV marketing department.

Petra wouldn't hear it. She actually knew who was behind it, or said she did—apparently some bored psychologist, a friend of a friend of her hipster dad, who'd ripped off the concept from the "S*** Happens" sloganeers. She went so far as to decide on her senior quote in the middle of our argument: "There are no original ideas"—Anonymous. I made the dumb mistake of pointing out that this wasn't really a quote; it was a cliché. "That's the whole point, Hen," she groaned, pitying my naïveté. "It's meta." Needless to say, I didn't get lucky that day.

Maybe that's why I wasn't all that upset about being fired by

Petra outside the Bimbo Lounge. But *that* was upsetting, the fact that nothing could upset me—not even this beautiful girl who had ditched me in the rain. At the time, I chalked it up to the old bully's rule of the playground: Punch an arm long enough, eventually that arm goes numb. Lord knows that my proverbial arm had been beaten senseless. Try to see it from my perspective. Or better yet, try to see it from *your* perspective: Here's this loser, and his sister has been missing for a year; his parents are slowly losing their minds; his grades have long since circled the drain; last night he forgot yet again to put his socks in the hamper . . . and now his girlfriend has abandoned him, too.

Does that sound self-pitying?

Good. I think I'm entitled to a little self-pity now and then.

There was an upside, though. Standing on that grim sidewalk—dripping wet, fired, and alone—I had six simultaneous epiphanies:

1. Petra is very shallow and self-obsessed. I'm better off without her.

2. Okay, that's a big lie. Petra is hot and smart and funny (in writing), and even if she's annoying sometimes, nobody is better off without a girl like that.

3. But the deed is done, so it's time to face facts: The only reason Petra went out with me was because she needed a bass player for PETRA.

4. PETRA was never a joke band, and I'm a terrible bass player . . . and, wait, there goes George Monroe into

the club. Hmm. As discussed, George shreds on bass, and he's also better looking than I am, and he's actually a really nice guy—I mean, we're not supertight or anything, but he's always been cool to me—and now I bet he's stealing my job and my girlfriend.

5. I want to be angry with George for this if it's true, but I'm not, and I'm not sure why (though it probably comes back to the old rule of the playground).

6. In spite of her shallow self-obsession, Petra is honest. She fired me because she needs a replacement, and I'm sure it's George—I mean, come on; what are the chances that he just showed up here?—and he can actually get into a Lower East Side club like the Bimbo Lounge, whereas I probably can't.

I glanced at the bouncer again. He was attempting to open an umbrella without much luck. I wondered about the pin on his lapel. Maybe *he* was the psychologist friend of a friend of Petra's dad. Maybe he'd once imagined himself to be a genius by ripping off the "S*** Happens" people and then came to the sad realization that he was nothing more than a plagiarist and was now forced to moonlight as a bouncer for the extra cash. Maybe, like me, he was a cautionary tale.

From inside, I heard the faint strains of Shakes the Clown's opener, a modified cover of the seventies soft-rock classic: "Feelings . . . nothing more than feelings . . ."

"Feelings . . . Barnyard hoedown feelings . . .

"Feelings . . . Prison hose-down feelings . . ."

There wasn't much point in hanging around. It was a ten-minute walk to the subway and a half-hour ride after that. Plus, I needed to make the Emma call.

Whenever I suffer, whenever I rejoice, whenever those occasions arise when I think I might be close to slipping closer to the abyss of insanity, I make a point to talk it all through with my next-door neighbor Emma Wood. Skinny, neurotic, ratty haired, reclusive Emma Wood—she is and always has been the only person who can convince me that I am, in fact, still sane. Or at least sane in comparison to her.

Emma lives at 598 Pacific Street. I live at 596. More than my next-door neighbor, however, Emma Wood has been my sort-of sister for the past decade. She assumed that role ever since my *real* sister—biologically, if nothing more—babysat the two of us at Emma's house after Emma moved in with her quiet mom and nut-job dad (more on him later).

This was a seminal event on many levels. Not only did Emma and I succeed in locking Sarah in the bathroom but we also ate all her dad's Jolly Ranchers and fed raw hamburger to Emma's cat, which grossed me out so much that I became a vegetarian, and I've stuck to it ever since—I swear, not a bite of meat in ten years, even at school. (The only animal product I eat are eggs; they're just too good with cheese to forgo.) And all the while, Sarah pounded furiously on the bathroom door and begged to be let out. In addition, as vengeance Sarah swore to destroy the Lego fort on top of my dresser and to slice to shreds Emma's entire stuffed animal collection, which she later held hostage at knifepoint. (The threats turned out to be empty.) It was the first time I'd ever gotten the best of Sarah. Unfortunately, it would also be the last, but that wasn't Emma's fault.

I hunched over my cell phone and dialed, fighting to shield the tiny keypad from the rain.

"Wow, that's so weird!" she answered.

"What is?"

"I was just going to call you," she said. "I now have proof that there is no God. The band Journey still exists. What label would carry them? It was bad enough when Mom told me that 'Lovin', Touchin', Squeezin'' was 'their' song. You know how much the wedding video traumatized me. But now they're actually going to pay to see the so-called reunited Journey in concert. It's June twenty-sixth. Anyway, Dad said I could bring you, and I was wondering if you wanted to go. I mean, for comic value—"

"Emma?" I interrupted. My teeth chattered. I was wet and miserable. I was on the Lower East Side of Manhattan, far from home. She knew all this.

"Yeah, I know. You don't remember who Journey is. I'll give you a hint. Picture my mom, circa 1983. Then start singing, 'Just a small town girl—'"

"No. She finally did it."

"Your mom actually burned your socks?" Emma hooted.

"No, Petra broke up with me. Then she kicked me out of her band. In that order."

14

"Oh," she said.

I frowned, my nose dripping. "That's all you have to say?"

"No. But it would have been a lot funnier if your mom burned your socks."

I sighed. "I guess you have a point."

"Hen, you can't get too upset about this," she warned. "Remember that ancient *Simpsons* episode, when Lisa said that the Chinese have the same word for both crisis and opportunity? This is a classic case of 'crisi-tunity'! You should make the most of it. Just like how Ozzy made the most of it when he was kicked out of Black Sabbath. Who's had the most lucrative solo career *ever*?" she finished rhetorically.

"Jermaine Jackson," I said.

"Very funny."

"Seriously, Emma, I thought you liked Petra."

"The person or the band?" She snorted. "Listen, Hen, I say a lot of stuff. I once said that her band might have a shot at making it big or whatever. But I didn't say the stuff you need to hear. Like how Petra always sneaks a peek at herself in any reflective surface, like an ATM screen or even a gypsy cab window."

"That's what I need to hear?" I asked, sloshing through a puddle.

"No, but she's raised self-obsession to an art form. And you had something she wanted."

I almost laughed. "What's that?"

"You have this edgy mystique," Emma said.

Then I did laugh. For a second, I forgot about the rain.

I even forgot about how the rain might short-circuit my cell phone and electrocute me. "You want to run that by me again? You're not making any sense."

"You're the guy whose sister disappeared, remember? Petra said it herself."

"Yeah, I remember," I said. "I'm the guy whose sister disappeared."

"You were even on the news."

Yes, Emma, I remember, I grumbled silently. *I was even on the news.*

And what a fifteen minutes of fame it was. About a week before school started in the fall, a twentysomething blond reporter—a real go-getter, at least judging from the amount of hair product and makeup she wore—showed up at our door with her trusty bearded cameraman sidekick, straight out of central casting. They arrived on the heels of the police's third and final visit, basically to ask the same question: Why would a smart, attractive, white (apparently even with our black president, America isn't still *quite* "postracial") twenty-two-year-old Ivy League grad vanish with four friends without any explanation? The response Mom and Dad gave to the reporter and her cameraman—which was the same response they'd given to the cops—was: "We have no idea. Yes, we are a close family. No, she doesn't have any skeletons in her closet. Neither do we. Yes, we are worried and shocked and blindsided and praying that she'll show up soon, safe and sound. . . ."

The twisted part? I knew better. Mom and Dad *did* know why Sarah had run away, and moreover, why she was wanted by law enforcement. And the *truly* criminal part? They refused to tell me. So did the cops, but for a different and much more understandable reason: They couldn't jeopardize an ongoing investigation.

No matter how hard I had begged my parents—and I'd begged in some small, subtle way every single day—they wouldn't budge. It was for my own good, they said. "Sarah can tell you herself, when she comes home." In the Hall of Fame of Unfairness-Coupled-with-Lousy-Parenting, that comment deserves its own gold plaque.

Anyway, the reporter and the cameraman wouldn't take the hint to leave. And just at the very moment Mom and Dad started screaming at "Blondie and the Beard" to "get the hell off our stoop!!!" (Mom actually addressed them in the third person as such), I strolled into camera range on my way home from the deli. There was a choice shot of me, with my jaw hanging open, looking like a lobotomy patient. It made both the six and eleven o'clock broadcasts, sandwiched right between the same two pieces about how the nightmarish economy was affecting the Chinese food delivery industry and a series of rapid-fire man-on-the-street interviews asking random people what they thought about the Steal Your Parents' Money stickers. (Best response: "I stole my mom's wallet this morning! Hi, Mom!")

There you have the short-lived Sarah Birnbaum media circus, in a nutshell.

Emma sighed on the other end. "Listen, Hen, this is going to sound harsh, but Petra never saw you for who you are. To her, you're just this guy with a runaway sister—a sister who's rumored to be a fugitive from the law, no less—so even though you don't realize it yourself, you do have this semicriminal aura, which is always great for a band. Plus, on a more practical level, you have a really kick-ass bass rig—"

"Petra did say she had feelings for me," I interrupted.

"Any dump*er* says that she still has 'feelings' for the dump*ee*, Hen," Emma groaned. "It's a perennial. It's in a thousand cheesy songs. It ranks just below 'It's not you; it's me' and 'I think we need a little time apart.' Which just goes to show you, Petra is not the creative genius she makes herself out to be. And even if her band *does* make it big—which they won't—they're going to end up being total crap. *You* deserve better. Speaking of which: What about this Journey concert? It's three weeks from tomorrow night. Wanna make a deal? If you come with me, I'll do something really nice for you, okay? *I'll* put your socks in the hamper."

"Um . . . I'll let you know," I said. "Bye, Emma." I closed the cell phone and shoved it back into my damp pocket.

Maybe Emma was right. Maybe the only reason Petra had gone out with me was because I was the "guy whose sister disappeared," and I had a kick-ass bass rig. The silly irony is that the only reason my parents bought me such a rig (a Mesa Boogie speaker with a custom Acoustic head, if that means anything to you) was because they felt guilty about having spent most of last year obsessing over Sarah and keeping me in the dark about why she was gone.

As if it even merits a mention, their extravagant expenditure did not make up for their incomprehensible behavior or for the fact that I have very little musical talent.

But that's not even the best part.

No: the sillier irony? The punch line? The wrap-up to this laugh-out-loud, million-hits-on-YouTube-worthy evening?

After a long, lonely subway ride back to Brooklyn (the train smelled), I arrived in the pouring rain to find a note dangling precariously from a piece of tape on the front door of the Birnbaum family brownstone.

Hen,

> *Guess what? Sarah came home!* ☺
>
> *Can you believe it? She made us swear not to tell anyone she's here. So you should probably throw this note in the garbage as soon as you read it.*
>
> *We're at the airport, picking her up. We tried to call you on the cell, but you must have been on the train. If she's not in need of immediate medical or psychiatric treatment, we'll be back at about 11:30, depending on traffic. But the expressway is always a nightmare, and who knows about Atlantic Ave.?*
> *Love you,*
> *Mom*

> *PS: There's some leftover Chinese in the fridge. We got you vegetable lo mein. Your favorite! But try not to finish it. Dad wants some.*

> *PPS: Try to clean your room a little, too, before we get home, okay? It would be nice for Sarah.*

CHAPTER TWO

A Big Favor

I did not try not to finish the vegetable lo mein. Nor did I try *to* finish it. I did not try to clean my room. I did not try anything.

The whole entire year I'd been *trying*—trying to make sense of Sarah's disappearing act and the peculiar, gaping hole it had left in my life; trying to make sense of why my parents wouldn't let me in on the secret—and every time I tried, I came up short. So: No more trying.

Why try to turn on the lights?

Sarah was coming home. *She* could turn on the lights.

Sarah is coming home, I repeated to myself, wondering if the words would carry more weight if I silently shouted them. They didn't.

Good. Once again, I could not feel a thing. Above all, I did not *try* to feel. I sat in the dark at the kitchen table. For a while, I stared at the blank spaces on the wall where the photos of Sarah had once hung. ("I can't bear to see her face in two dimensions," Mom had wailed once with far too much drama, even for her.) The seconds ticked by. I knew, objectively, that each tick brought me closer to a reunion with a long-lost sister who had abandoned her family—and now, judging from the tone of the note on the door, was somehow getting off entirely scot-free. Should I be at all mad?

Maybe if she spills the beans the second she walks in the door, I shouldn't be.

Ticktock, ticktock . . .

But no . . . maybe I *should* be mad, because she always got away with everything, even before she split. Did part of me always suspect she'd come back?

Ticktock, ticktock . . .

I wasn't mad, though. At least not now. Hooray for me.

Maybe if I played the whole fiasco over in my head again . . .

Graduation day at Columbia . . . Sarah's square cap flying up into the sunshine, the cheers, the euphoric laughter . . . and she was graduating with honors, no less. Everything should have been wonderful, right? The ceremony marked the first time Mom and Dad had cried real-live tears of joy, which, if you want to know the truth, was sort of disturbing. But then she broke the news: instead of sticking to the summer plan of living at home with her spanking-new Ivy League adulthood, she was slinking off to an illegal sublet in a Chinatown tenement with Gabriel and her college roommate, Madeline . . . and then Mom and Dad stopped crying and got pissed. As well they should have. Not because the sublet was illegal, but mostly because Sarah still kept insisting that she and Gabriel were just "pals." *Pals?* Please. She'd talked about Gabriel incessantly ever since freshman year. ("He's so funny!" "He plays bass!" "He's in this hilarious band!" No, Mom and Dad, that doesn't sound like a pal to me, either.) Still, they let her go without a fight. What about living at home to save money?

But it wasn't the Birnbaum family coffers I cared about. Selfishly—even though I never said as much out loud—I needed Sarah to provide that essential buffer between my lunatic parents and me.

Some examples of why it was helpful, if not crucial, to have Sarah around:

1. **The "[Hen] discovered girls!" incident.** Three Decembers ago, Mom and Dad decided to proclaim to the world that I'd entered puberty. In print. Paragraph two of their holiday card read: "Hen asked us to buy him an electric bass. Between that and the amount of time he's been spending alone in the bathroom, we've come to the obvious conclusion: He's discovered girls!" Sarah luckily got a hold of the final draft before it went out, adding: "Irv has discovered the joys of Viagra!"

(Untrue, but it did prevent Mom and Dad from going ahead with the mass mailing. One hundred fifty people would have seen it, including teachers at Franklin.) To this day, Mom and Dad claim they still don't understand why I'd been so horrified.

2. **The time Mom and Dad attempted to sell all my vegetarian literature and snack food on eBay.** This coincided with Mom's slamming the door in Sarah's face the night of my fourteenth birthday. She'd foiled their plan to use the money they'd made from the eBay sale to take the four of us to Peter Luger Steak House (difficult, anyway, as they'd netted $14.00). Sarah was outraged, because she'd guessed rightly that it was all part of a vast conspiracy to get me to eat meat. For reasons that still elude me, Mom and Dad lump vegetarianism in with "deviant behaviors"—their words—such as cross-dressing, online gambling, and porn collecting. They also believe that it's an easy fix: Upon seeing a succulent slab of beef, I will naturally lose all control and bury my face in it. After Mom slammed the door on her, Sarah screamed at them that they were crazy and evil, grabbed me, and stormed out. We dined alone at a vegan restaurant in Chelsea. Mom and Dad later apologized, but grudgingly. Who knows? If they'd tried to take me to Peter Luger this past year, I might be gnawing on a T-bone right now.

3. **The reason we all have our own cell phones.** Dad, in one of his more paranoid moments, told us to stop using our house landline. He believes that the government is spying on us. (I really, really wish I were joking.) According to him, our neighbor Mr. Aziz is on some sort of terror watch list, and anyone who shops at his deli near the Bergen Street F train stop is now under suspicion, too. All untrue, as Sarah confirmed simply by asking Mr. Aziz himself if he'd ever had any trouble with the government. (The closest he'd ever come was trying to return a tax refund that was too big.) But she'd pretended to go along, provided that Dad buy each of us our own cell phone. He'd agreed. Stooge!

What else? The examples could fill a book . . . but there you have a snapshot of Mom and Dad's madness and some of their more colorful wrongs.

Let's face it, though: *They* wanted Sarah around last summer as much as I did. Why hadn't they pleaded with her to reconsider the sublet? At the time I'd chalked it up to some weird phase they were going through, a letting-go-of-their-firstborn type of thing, an unwanted rite of middle-aged passage . . . and Sarah kept insisting that she just wanted to "have fun" before she started the Columbia School of Social Work in the fall. But, what—she couldn't live at home with us and still have fun on her own? No, she'd rather shaft us and be "autonomous" . . . And don't forget the volunteer job at that homeless shelter in Tribeca, New Beginnings, all to prove how noble, how thoughtful, how *grown-up* she was—as if it somehow justified shacking up with her "pal" Gabriel in a sketchy part of town that reeked of old fish.

Then she was gone. And with her, Gabriel and Madeline. Plus two more friends from Columbia, guys who were in Gabriel's band: Rich and Tony. Without a warning. Without a good-bye. One day they were here; the next, they weren't. They'd left zero evidence that they'd ever existed in the first place. Actually, that isn't quite true. The cops later told us that they'd left behind a new air conditioner to replace the one they'd broken plus the rest of the money for the summer sublet.

How noble! How thoughtful! How grown-up!

Ticktock, ticktock . . .

The front door lock clicked.

My heart began to pound. I tried to make it stop beating so loudly. I couldn't. The heart is an inattentive and all-around-annoying little organ. The lungs, generally obedient, are much easier to get along with. I held my breath.

Sarah is home.

The door opened. People entered.

"Hen?" Mom called. "Hello? Hen, are you home? Hen . . ." The door closed. "For God's sake, Irv, why is the door unlocked?"

Three pairs of footsteps approached.

Sarah is home.

I wanted to appear relaxed, stoic. I fidgeted in my chair.

Someone flicked on the kitchen lights—

And there she was. The prodigal daughter, returned.

I was expecting her to look different somehow. I was expecting her to look filthy and scrawny, her black hair tangled and even messier than Emma's from months of living out of Dumpsters. I was not expecting her outfit to proclaim: Life as a runaway sure was sweet! Maybe I'd just been being naïve (again). Mom and Dad had picked her up at JFK International Airport. Rock stars flew in and out of that airport. Rock stars as well dressed as she was. Rock stars as *stylishly* dressed. Just *look* at her: suited up in black pants and a black tank top: neatly pressed, hip, and matching . . . She had a tan, too. Her face was goofy and bug-eyed, just as it had always been.

"Hi, Hen," she said with a smile.

A smile? I thought to myself. Really? A prisoner freed from an unjust incarceration could have smiled. A cancer patient in remission could have smiled. But Sarah? Her voice was the same, too. Entitled. Upbeat. I stared at her. I stared for a very long time.

Mom and Dad know everything, and they're smiling, too.

A hint, anyone? Hello?

Then I remembered: I was done trying.

Without a word, I stood and marched past my newly reunited family, up the stairs to my third-floor bedroom.

"Hen?" Mom called after me. "Hen? What is it?"

Sarah is home.

*   *   *

26

I couldn't hide forever. I could make it through the night, sure, but tomorrow Sarah would still be in this house, with her healthy tan. (Or maybe she wouldn't.)

An hour after she'd arrived, I was still in bed, staring angrily at various parts of my room. But wait: Was it even *my room?* Everything I called my own had changed after Sarah had run away—either abruptly or in subtle increments—but, no, this was not the room that belonged to the Hen Birnbaum I'd been last July, the one with an older sister who could be counted on and sniped at and taken for granted.

First, there was the Lego fort. Until August, it had been sitting on top of my dresser, since the very day Sarah had threatened to destroy it. Maybe I was a little old to display a Lego fort on top of my bureau (though it *was* cool in an infantile sort of way, a replica of the Tower of London), but if Sarah hadn't run away, I guarantee it still would be sitting there. I'd destroyed it myself the first time the cops had questioned Mom and Dad—the night I knew for sure that Sarah had run away for real. It hadn't started as destruction, more of a dismantling. I'd gritted my teeth as I pulled the plastic pieces apart, but then I just went ultraviolent. Pitiful and childish, yes, but tossing the little plastic pieces everywhere felt pretty awesome; and they'd sat on my floor for days.

Then there was my erstwhile Dandy Warhols poster. Sarah had given it to me two years ago, right after I bought my bass. She'd heard that the Dandy Warhols had built some sort of huge recording studio/playland called the Odditorium, where they hosted huge gatherings with their friends. She'd told me that they hung out and jammed and recorded new songs and made videos—whatever they felt like—and she hoped that I ended up in band like that: a freewheeling, bohemian collective of tight pals where "the act of creating was more important than the paycheck." (She actually managed to say this without sounding ditzy or pretentious, too—how, I'm still not sure.) The poster had managed to stay up on my wall until late December. But then I'd had the bad luck of catching one of those end-of-the-year countdowns on the one decent radio station left in New York City, and they'd chosen the Dandy Warhols' "We Used to Be Friends" as song number 387 of the top 1,000 alternative rock songs of all time . . . and upon hearing it, I'd ripped the poster off the wall and torn it to shreds. That had felt pretty awesome, too—

There was a knock.

"Hen?" Sarah asked. "Can I come in?"

Without waiting for an answer, she pushed the door forward. I turned to the blank spot on the wall, then back to her. She *did* look a little scrawnier than she had last summer, now that I thought about it.

"Your room looks different," she remarked.

"So do you," I said.

"I guess I do. Can I sit down?"

"If you want. Just don't mess anything up on my desk." It was an old line I'd used with her many times, and I instantly regretted it.

"It's okay. I'll stand." She paused. "Hen, this is hard. . . . I'm not going to BS you. I can't tell you why I ran away. Not yet. I do want you to know something, though. It had nothing to do with you. Okay?"

"Okay."

"Do you believe me? It's important that you believe me."

"I didn't think it had anything to do with me," I said.

She stared down at her expensive-looking black shoes.

"Anything else?" I asked.

"Just— You can't tell anyone that I'm home," she said. "I mean, you can tell Emma, because I know you're going to tell her anyway, but you have to make her swear that she won't tell anyone."

"Got it. You're not home. Is that it?"

"Hen, come on," she murmured as if she were a victim.

"What?" I said.

"Can't you talk to me?" she asked.

I closed my eyes. "About what? No offense, but I'm a little tired. I've had a pretty crappy day. In your absence, my life did manage to go on. And right now, it's at a low point. It has nothing to do with *you*, though."

Sarah sighed.

"I'm not BSing you, either," I added. "My girlfriend dumped me."

"Really?" she said. "I'm sorry, Hen. I am."

"Like I said, it has nothing to do with you," I repeated.

"What's her name?" she asked.

"For Christ's sake, Sarah!" I flipped over, briefly mashing my face into the pillow, then glared at her. "I don't want to talk about it."

"I'm sorry. Umm . . ." She brushed her hair behind her ear, an old nervous gesture. "Listen, I know this probably isn't the best time, but I want you to do me a favor."

"A favor?"

Sarah really *was* home. And that was it. The spell was broken. I was no longer in danger of crying.

"Yeah," she said. She laughed sadly—the way she used to laugh when she was in trouble with Mom and Dad. "This is going to sound really bad, Hen."

I had to laugh, too. "As compared to what?"

"My friend Gabriel came back home with me. I mean, to New York."

For a horrible instant, I wondered if that meant our house. But, no, it couldn't. Sarah wouldn't have pushed her luck that far.

"Good for him," I said.

"And, see, he wants to try to get his life back on track. He needs structure . . . a new purpose. Something positive. He says he wants to start teaching kids how to play bass. You remember that he plays bass, too, don't you?"

"Nope. Can't say that I do."

"You remember Gabriel though, right?" she asked.

"I remember that when I met him, he said he liked the theme song from the TV show *Friends*. I decided to stop paying attention to him after that."

Sarah laughed again.

"I wasn't trying to be funny," I said.

"No . . . it's just, Gabriel was in a *band* called Friends," she explained, as if this somehow made sense. "They were a nine-ties nostalgia act. They opened every show with that song. But anyway, I was thinking, since you play bass, too, maybe you could be his first student? It would mean so much to him, and to me. Besides, Mom and Dad mentioned you were probably going to get some summer tutors, anyway. So why not make Gabriel your first? I bet your bass playing would get a lot better—"

"Sarah?"

"Yeah?"

"I don't know who you are. But I'd like you to leave."

"Hen, please—"

"You don't understand, do you?" I asked.

"Understand what?"

"Anything!" My face burned. I clutched the pillow. "How do you know I even need bass lessons, Sarah? For all you know, I could have become the next Flea in the past year. For all you know, I'm a superstar. For all you know, I should be giving *Gabriel* bass lessons."

"I'm so sorry, you're right." She backed out the door. "Wait. Flea's the guy from the Red Hot Chili Peppers, right?"

"It doesn't matter." I buried myself under the covers. "Forget it. Just— Please turn off the light on your way out."

"Okay, Hen." I could hear her shoes scuffling, then a pause. She flicked off the light switch. "I'll let you sleep. Just one more thing: Gabriel is crashing in the East Village right now, so when you go to his place, be sort of careful, okay? The police or the FBI might still be looking for him. Everything is going to get cleared up soon; I promise. That's why we came back. And I know Mom and Dad are waiting for me to tell you . . . but that's another story. Just try not to attract so much attention to yourself at first, okay? It's not a big deal; things are in motion . . . just, if you see something weird—like guys in black suits with wires in their ears—you know, go back home and call to reschedule the lesson. Okay?"

"Sure," I replied, not knowing or caring what she was talking about. "Anything you say. Welcome to the Birnbaum house, whoever you are."

CHAPTER THREE

Diary of My Life on the Lam, by Gabriel Stern

When I awoke the next morning, I felt a surprising calm. I'd slept well. Miraculously well: It was a heavy, black, dreamless sleep. I yawned and stretched, refreshed. Not that I'd forgotten what had happened. Of course not. My first thoughts were of Sarah, then of Petra, and then of the horrible confluence of events, the great cosmic practical joke that had been played on me with the coincidence of Sarah's reappearing and Petra's firing, all on the same rainy night.

Still, I was okay. The proverbial arm had indeed been beaten senseless.

I felt *good*.

So. My sister wanted me to take bass lessons from a fellow

fugitive? No problem. Even less of a problem than that she couldn't tell me why she'd run away or why she'd suddenly come back—or why my parents were still mysteriously silent on the subject. It was the opposite of a problem; it was a crisitunity. If I took bass lessons from Gabriel, then maybe *he* could tell me what happened, and I could also gain the necessary musical skills for Petra to rehire me for PETRA.

Look out, George Monroe!

I hopped out of bed and marched to the bathroom. I brushed my teeth and threw on some frayed old jeans and a plain white T-shirt. I packed up my bass in its case. With a broad smile, I sauntered downstairs, where—*how wonderful!*—my newly reunited family was silently eating a scrambled egg breakfast in our sunlit kitchen. All of them looked haggard, worse than the night before, Sarah worst of all. Of course, Mom and Dad always looked haggard. Both generally gave off a vibe of quiet, stooped suffering that was a lot more nineteenth-century Siberian shtetl than twenty-first-century Brooklyn brownstone. They were still wearing the same clothes. Good for them! I'd slept in my clothes last night, too. Only, I'd had the good sense to change.

"Hi, Hen," Mom said, looking up from her plate of eggs. "Are you okay?"

"Never better," I said.

"What's with the bass?" Dad asked. "Where are you going?"

"I'm going to take bass lessons from Sarah's friend Gabriel,"

I said. "Didn't Sarah tell you?"

"Excuse me?" Mom asked.

She and Dad exchanged horrified glances. My smile widened.

Sarah bolted up and grabbed me by the shoulders. She whisked me down the hall and out the front door. I didn't bother fighting back. Her painful sisterly grip was just as unforgiving as I remembered. "What are you doing?" she said.

I shrugged, breathing in the morning air. Last night's rain had cleared away the stickiness. The tree in front of Emma's house was as green and leafy as I'd ever seen it.

"Hen?" Sarah pressed. "I'm not joking. What's going on?"

"I'm going to my bass lesson," I answered. "Wait, you *did* call Gabriel and set it up, didn't you? You said it yourself. For reasons you can't tell me, Gabriel needs to get his life back on track. And I definitely need tutoring. My grades sucked this year. It's so funny: My college adviser said that taking bass lessons from a fugitive would increase my chances of getting into Harvard."

"Shh." Sarah peered back into the house, chewing her lip. "All right. I screwed up. I owe you. I'll call him right now."

"Who?"

"Gabriel," she said.

I opened my mouth to stop her.

Was she really . . . ? Yes, she *was*. She was calling Gabriel on her cell phone.

She ran downstairs to the sidewalk in front of Emma's

house and engaged in a frantic, hushed conversation. The only word I heard clearly was: "Gabriel?"

I shifted my weight, wondering what I was doing.

"Sarah?" I whispered, but she didn't hear.

Mom burst out of the door, holding a tinfoil cube.

"What's that?" I asked.

"I made you a whole-wheat egg sandwich for the road." Mom shoved it into my hands. "You may be a vegetarian. I may have cooked you your own separate main courses for going on a decade now, even on the High Holidays—out of the goodness of my heart—but you're not going to start skipping breakfast, like your sister did. You're not going to do *anything* like your sister did. Somehow, somewhere, *somebody* has to make some rules. And somebody has to stick to them!"

What happened next was a little hazy.

There were flashes: Mom, slamming the door . . . Sarah, giving me directions to Gabriel's East Village crash pad . . . me, gobbling down the breakfast sandwich . . .

My memory only sharpens with what happened when I stopped outside the Bergen Street subway entrance and dialed Emma.

"Wow, that's so weird!" she answered.

"What is?"

"I was just going to call you," she said.

"Why? What's up?"

"I know we made a deal never to talk about dreams, but last

night, I went to bed early and dreamed that your sister came home."

Without thinking, I hung up and shoved the phone into my pocket. I stopped, clutching a sweaty palm against my white T-shirt. I clung to the strap of my bass case as if it were a life preserver.

Seconds later, my phone rang.

I took a deep breath. Okay. No reason to freak out. This was Emma. This kind of stuff happened. It was nothing more than a bizarre coincidence. Maybe she'd seen my parents' soggy note on our door. But even if not, why should I even care about what she dreamed? Dreams meant nothing—we'd *decided* that. Still, my hands began to shake as I fished the phone out of my pocket. I decided not to let her get the edge on the conversation. Instead I initiated and rambled, Emma style: "Hi, Emma— yeah, listen, I'm sorry I hung up on you. But I really can't talk right now. Your dream came true, okay? Your dream came true. And I'm sorry if you have plans, but can you block some time for me this afternoon? I think I might be on the verge of . . . I don't know. I see a lot of jabbering involved."

She took a deep breath and spoke soothingly. "Of course. As long as you promise you'll never hang up on me again. Bye, Hen."

Gabriel's East Village crash pad wasn't quite what I expected.

For one thing, I expected the building to be a little more . . . well, *ghetto*—something closer to Sonic Rehearsal Studios.

But there wasn't even any graffiti on the redbrick wall. The glass doors were relatively shiny, and there was a sparkling new intercom system. I stood outside for several minutes, debating whether or not to ring. Sarah told me he was in 1B, the only apartment without a name label. I'd come all this way, and I didn't want to go home anytime soon, so . . . Screw it. I pressed the button.

The buzzer rang instantly.

When the door to 1B cracked open, I was even more surprised. Gabriel's place wasn't crawling with cops and FBI guys, which was what I'd been secretly hoping for. I guess it *did* look like a crash pad for fugitives. Either that or as if a movie set designer had been hired to create a "monkish, ascetic interior." It definitely wasn't the kind of place where a well-adjusted human being would want to spend more than a few days.

My eyes zeroed in on his bass, perched on a stand next to an unmade futon. Unfortunately, it seemed to confirm my suspicion that Gabriel Stern was a jackass.

A bass, like a high school locker, can say a lot about its proprietor. I own a cream-colored 1976 Fender Precision that I have chosen not to desecrate in reverence both for 1976 (the year the Sex Pistols and the Clash broke) and for how I bought it on eBay for only $250: the greatest steal of all time in the history of the world. It is not an advertisement for my personality, however. Gabriel owned a custom Ken Smith, for which he'd probably paid well over a thousand dollars. Everything about it said "I'm trying too hard." The body was smothered in stickers from the nineties, a clutter of grunge bands (remember Mudhoney?); not-quite-gangsta rappers (remember Naughty by Nature?); an official *Friends* cast photo (Get it? It's kitschy!); and, what do you know, one big exception right between the pickups: STEAL YOUR PARENTS' MONEY.

There wasn't any clutter in the apartment, though. Aside from the bass and bedding there was just a cheap practice amp, plus a two-foot-high stack of bound manuscripts next to the door. No dirty dishes or empty bottles or cigarette butts; no stereo, TV, or computer, or even (worst-case scenario) firearms . . . all of which I'd half expected to find given Gabriel's postcollegiate meltdown (if that's what it was). He looked awful, too. His blond hair was a mess, and he was about twenty-five pounds heavier than when I'd seen him last at that fateful graduation. He was wearing the same outfit I was: jeans and a plain white T-shirt.

"Hey, Hen," he said. "I really appreciate your coming—"

"My sister thinks I need bass lessons," I interrupted. "She's right. I stink."

He closed the door behind us. "So what else did your sister say?"

I was beginning to regret my decision to come here. What if the cops or FBI *did* show up? Would I be arrested, too?

"Nothing," I grumbled. "Look, why did you and my sister run away?" I demanded, mostly out of nervousness. Best to get the important stuff out of the way.

He laughed. The puffy circles under his eyes twitched. "I'm

sorry. I can't tell you that. Look, why don't we jam a little? I'll take the rhythm, you take the melody."

I turned away from him. "I don't feel like playing," I confessed. "This was a bad idea. I just came here to piss off my sister in front of my parents. I should leave."

"No, no," Gabriel insisted. His voice was hoarse. "Stick around. Come on, you came here all the way from Brooklyn. We don't have to play. We can just hang out. Ask me something. Anything . . . you know—aside from why your sister and I ran away."

I glared at him. "Were you really in a band called Friends?"

"Yeah." His face brightened. "Remember the show?"

"Sort of." In truth: Emma and I sometimes watched *Friends* reruns when we were bored and nothing else was on—and, yes, sometimes we even laughed. There was no way in hell I'd tell *him* that, though.

"The band was more than a tribute to the show," he said. "It was a tribute to the word itself. When we were little kids, 'friend' wasn't a verb. You didn't 'friend' someone. You *had* friends. It was only a noun. It didn't multitask." He sighed dramatically. "It was a simpler time, Hen."

Jesus. He looked at me as if he expected me to laugh. The silence between us stretched awkwardly.

"Um . . . anything else?" he said, clearing his throat.

"Yeah. Were you and my sister ever involved? Are you involved now?"

He smiled widely at the question. It was the same sort of

smile I'd given my parents this morning when they'd asked me what I was doing with my bass case. His bloodshot blue eyes didn't waver. He looked at peace, like a grizzled statue of the Buddha. I wanted to punch him. "There's no easy answer to that," he said. "Have you ever had certain thoughts about a girl who's just your friend?"

"No," I lied.

"Interesting." Gabriel shrugged. "In my experience, if you're a straight male and you're close with a girl, it's a thought that crosses your mind, no matter what. It may be a fleeting thought, but it always happens. Maybe just once. Maybe a thousand times."

"What are you, a shrink?"

He laughed. "No, but I could use one. You know of any? Kidding. Look, man, I know it's early, but I'm going to fix a drink. You want anything? A Bloody Mary? I won't tell Sarah."

I watched him disappear around the corner into the kitchen. His bare feet slapped on the shiny wooden floor. My breath quickened. I had a choice: I could stay and endure this excruciating torture, or I could bolt. My eyes fell to the pile of manuscripts. The clear plastic covering reminded me of Sarah's old term papers.

DIARY OF MY LIFE ON THE LAM
BY GABRIEL STERN
Contact number: 347 555 7809
Email: gsternfugitive@webmail.com

I snatched the top copy off the pile.

"Hen?" Gabriel called. "You sure you don't want a Bloody Mary?"

"Actually, I think I do," I said.

"Cool!"

I heard the refrigerator door open. And with that, I shoved Gabriel's manuscript into the front pocket of my bass case and ran from the apartment. I didn't stop running until I'd reached the nearest subway station, ten blocks away—my heart pounding loudly and even my normally obedient lungs disobeying the unspoken command to mellow out.

Only later at Emma's, sitting on the edge of her bed next to her, could I confess to the theft—and only *after* I'd hashed out the drama of my sister's surprise return and the ensuing madness of this morning.

"Hen!" she cried. "You've never stolen anything in your life."

I hung my head in shame. "I know."

Emma's room is the kind of place that breeds confession. Or maybe "confession" is the wrong word; it breeds honesty. There's no mystery, either. It's a pure place. I've always liked her room more than mine, even before Sarah's disappearance, because it never changes. She still has those same threadbare stuffed animals on her bed (the ones Sarah had threatened to slice to shreds), those same posters of forgotten boy bands on her walls, with their eyes and teeth blacked out and horns markered on their heads.

"Hen, you need to bring back that diary now," Emma warned me. "Don't read it. It's not yours. You might not like what you find out. Look, let's make a pact—"

"No; no more pacts. I *have* to read it. Nobody will tell me why Sarah ran away. Not Gabriel, not my parents, and definitely not *her*. The way she's acting . . . It's like she thinks that if I find out, it'll have some adverse affect on my mental health. As if my mental health could get worse. And if I don't find out what happened, I really *will* lose it. I'll read it all tonight, and then bring it back to Gabriel first thing in the morning. Better yet, I'll call him as soon as I get home and apologize for bolting—I'll make up some excuse; you know, it was too weird or too soon after Sarah got home or whatever—and reschedule the bass lesson for tomorrow. And as soon as I get there, I'll just slip the manuscript back where I found it, right on top of the stack with all the others. He'll never even know it was missing."

Emma sighed. "You better hope he doesn't. He's a fugitive from the law. I bet he keeps pretty close track of his possessions."

"He won't miss it," I said, mostly to myself. "Don't worry."

She didn't say anything. She ran a hand through her ratty hair.

"What?" I said.

"Worrying is *your* specialty, Hen," she said. "You just don't know it."

CHAPTER FOUR
Balinese Demons

I arrived home that afternoon to find my father at the dining room table, swamped in a sea of crumpled receipts and jabbing at an oversize calculator.

Dad insists on doing his own taxes, which I'm pretty sure is a weird thing to do. He also cuts his own hair, which depending on his luck and wardrobe alternately makes him look like an absentminded professor or a homeless person. He is the only adult I know who does either.

Last spring I even conducted a little survey to determine if doing one's taxes was, in fact, as weird as I thought it was. Of the six adults I'd queried, every single one said that they paid someone else to do their taxes for them. Four (all teachers at Franklin) asked if my dad was an accountant, and laughed uncomfortably when I told them he wasn't. Three, including Mr. Aziz, added that doing one's own taxes was an invitation to get audited. One—Emma's father, who can always be counted on for something offensive (like I said, more on him later)—said simply that Dad was a moron.

It isn't pride that drives Dad, and it's something beyond stubbornness; it's the belief that what makes *him* self-sufficient makes everyone else foolish, misguided, lazy, or all three. It's admirable in a way, which I guess is what keeps the rest of us from complaining when he takes over the dining room four times a year and turns it into his own private little H&R Block. (The dining room table is the only surface in the house large enough to accommodate all the paperwork.) On the plus side, it also prevents him and Mom from entertaining. During those tense little stretches leading up to the IRS tax deadline every third month, I know I won't be hearing, for example: "Hen, can you dust, vacuum, and set the table for five with the good china? Saul Levy's hernia operation was a success and we want to have him and Myrna over to celebrate."

To be honest, the sight of Dad slaving over the familiar mess made me feel sort of relieved. Sarah's return was not cause for a breakdown in the household routine. Mom was right: There were rules, and we could all stand to stick to them, even the bizarre self-imposed ones. Sarah's *disappearance* hadn't prevented him from doing his own taxes, so why should he stop now that she was back?

"That was quite a long bass lesson," Dad remarked as I shut the door.

Uh-oh. Had Gabriel already discovered what I'd done and called the house, looking for his stolen property? "I stopped by Emma's on the way home," I said defensively, glancing down the hall toward the empty kitchen. "Where's Sarah?"

"Out back with your mother. She says the garden is falling apart."

For some reason, that irritated me. Who was Sarah to say that the garden was falling apart? And so what if it was? What had she expected, that we would all become expert horticulturists to make up for her absence? *Screw the garden,* I felt like saying. I didn't know why I was so upset, but I found myself wishing we'd blacktopped the backyard and outlawed gardening altogether, in any form, period.

Dad leaned back in his chair. "Hen, what do you see yourself doing when you graduate from college?" he asked, peering at me over the rims of his glasses.

The question caught me off guard. "What do you mean?"

He nodded toward the bass slung across my back. "Do you see yourself being a professional musician?"

I didn't answer right away. Dad almost never asked about my plans for adulthood. Any rare discussion of my future usually occurred at mealtimes and was pretty much limited to Dad's insistence that I give up vegetarianism. ("You don't want people not to trust you," he'd told me in one of his more memorable non sequiturs—as if honesty and, say, hamburger, were inextricably linked.) Obviously, this peculiar line of questioning had something to do with Sarah's reappearance; I just wasn't sure how.

"I don't know," I said finally. "Why do you ask?"

"I suppose I'd just like to know how seriously you take playing the bass," he said.

"*You're* the one who bought me that great bass rig," I replied, feeling defensive again. "I have to take it pretty seriously, right?"

"Do you see yourself applying to a music school, like Juilliard, or that one in Boston . . . ?" He tapped his chin.

"Berklee?"

"Yes."

I glanced up the stairwell, wishing I were upstairs already. "I don't know. Probably not. You have to pass an audition to get in. I don't think I'd qualify."

"Do you think taking bass lessons with Sarah's friend might help?"

I laughed. Dad's pensive expression didn't change. "Um, I doubt it," I said. "You know, I really don't have to take lessons with him if you don't want me to. I'll look for some summer tutors first thing tomorrow."

"The time for finding summer tutors was back in March," Dad said.

I kept quiet, not wanting to get into another argument about what should have been done in March, especially during what Emma now calls my Lost Weekend. Dad had been invited to attend a freelancer's conference in Palm Beach, Florida (fun!) and Mom decided to tag along. Before they left, they charged me with a) finding summer tutors to help get my math and science grades back up, b) doing my laundry, and c) weeding the garden. The date of the conference was March 23, which coincidentally happened to be Sarah's birthday. Unfortunately, being left home alone for this conspicuously uncelebrated occasion depressed me so much that I sat in front of the TV for two days straight—not only accomplishing none of my appointed tasks but also allowing an ant problem in our kitchen to go unchecked. The exterminator ended up costing more than $400. Mom and Dad's subsequent freak-out marked the first time Mom threatened to burn my socks, in fact.

Dad exhaled deeply. "If these bass lessons are legitimately helping you achieve your goal of being a professional bassist, it's worth the risk," he said.

"The risk?" I repeated.

"Sarah and her friends . . . Well, they're technically fugitives until certain legal matters get straightened out. That's all I can tell you. And aiding and abetting criminals is not something I generally condone; but, like I said, I'm willing to let the circumstances slide for the time being. God knows I've let a lot worse slide this past year."

I slung the bass case off my back and propped it up against the stairwell banister. "Dad, are you okay?" I asked. I figured this question was better than the ones I felt like shouting at the top of my lungs, which were: *Why is that all you can tell me?*

What have you let slide? What is the big freaking deal? She's back, goddammit!!

"I'm fine," he said. "Why do you ask?"

"I don't know. Things are sort of weird, aren't they?"

"I'm not sure exactly what you mean, but I assume you're talking about Sarah's surprise homecoming. I guess I'd just like to see people in this household taking some responsibility for their futures. If professional bass playing isn't your goal—"

"It's just a hobby, Dad," I interrupted. "Playing an instrument is good for you."

"Yes, well." He pushed his glasses up his nose and turned his attention back to his taxes. "Like I said, if you *don't* intend on becoming a professional musician, I'd skip the lessons. Use your free time this summer to find a job or an internship that will help get your foot in the door of whatever you *do* intend to pursue as a profession."

I blinked. This odd little chat was fast degenerating into the realm of the creepy. Did he really expect me to have any idea what I wanted to "pursue as a profession"? Had he been dead certain that he'd wanted to be a freelance managerial consultant (I'm still not sure what that even is) when *he* was sixteen? Maybe he had. Whatever. If he couldn't tell me what was really bothering him—and I doubted very much it had anything to do with my employment status—then we were done.

"Fine, I'll look for a job, okay?" I said, grabbing my bass and scurrying upstairs. Odd: A long time ago, this would have been exactly the kind of nonsensical conversation that Sarah would have jumped right into on my behalf. I suddenly missed her more than ever, and she was right out back.

"You don't have to play the martyr here, Hen," Dad called after me.

I almost smiled, pausing on the top step. "What's that supposed to mean?"

"You sound bitter," he said.

"Bitter? Really? That's funny. Because I'm totally not."

I waited for him to laugh. Or something. He didn't. Which pretty much clinched what I'd already suspected: Now that Sarah was home, the lines of communication in the Birnbaum household had disintegrated completely.

Once I was alone, it took me a minute to muster the courage to remove Gabriel's manuscript from my bass case pouch. The plastic cover trembled slightly in my hands. It took me another minute to open it, even though I'd locked the door and hidden myself in bed half under the blanket and sheets. I was careful not to make a sound. My heart thumped loudly as I turned to the first page.

October 10
Recently my life has become a series of broken promises to myself.

I've promised to exercise, for one thing. I've gained fifteen pounds in 122 days. True, I'm not fat yet. I verged on emaciated in college. But I'm definitely more unkempt.

I should probably promise myself to get a haircut, too, or at least to shower more often. But it's hard to stay motivated.

In theory, there's no reason to stay motivated. I'm twenty-two. I call Puerto Plata, the Dominican Republic, my home, and it's sunny and seventy-five all year, except for the rainy season. I don't pay taxes. I'll never have to work. But on some level, I keep trying to tell myself that I'm also sick of excuses. I think maybe my father's skewed values have rubbed off on me more than I would like to admit—primarily the belief that hard work, regardless of its purpose or end, is the key to a guilt-free existence.

I smiled faintly. I could almost relate to the last part. But I wasn't sure if that was good or bad. The less I had in common with Gabriel, the better—on many, many levels. I skipped ahead a few pages.

October 23

Pouring a glass of whiskey at 4 P.M. every single day has become crucial to maintaining a precarious ability to relax. It's not the whiskey itself, although that helps. It's the act. It's watching that luscious amber liquid flow into the glass precisely as the hour hand and second hand overlap, pointing skyward in unison. I can't have it any other way.

I keep the whiskey on the mantel in the living room, in the exact center of the house, in a windowless cell that was originally built as a shrine for the Hindu god Ganesh. To get there, I have to walk through several narrow corridors, down two ramps, and up at least one partial spiral staircase. There are four spiral staircases altogether.

The journey takes exactly thirty-four seconds. My bedroom is on what I suppose could be called the second floor, though there are no "floors" in the true sense of the word; there are levels at varying heights. The house isn't designed for ease of movement. It isn't designed to be comfy or homey. It's designed specifically to repel leyaks: *Balinese demons who assume the form of monkeys, birds, and occasionally headless bodies.*

The odd construction made me pretty anxious at first. It took me some practice and time (thirty-two days) to master every single distance, from any room to any other, down to the second. Now I'm used to it. The distance-to-time ratio is firmly ingrained. But the worry still lingers: Will I be late?

If I am, I will have to pay the consequences. What worries me more than anything is the terrible unknown catastrophe that will inevitably occur if I screw up.

I paused for a second, confused. Was this a real-live diary, or something Gabriel had made up as he went along? It didn't read like a diary. I wasn't sure *what* it read like. A bad novel? I squirmed in bed, wishing I could ask Sarah if any of this were true. Funny: Emma was right, but not for the reasons she'd imagined. The manuscript wasn't bursting with any horrifying secrets or acts of depravity. I still couldn't figure out what Sarah and her friends had actually *done*.

I turned to the next page.

October 24

Today I raise my glass to toast our home's original owner: a middle-aged heroin dealer from Bali named Raj Bhutto. He planned to move to the Dominican Republic because he feared deadly reprisals of two kinds: the first being from rival dealers, the second being from the spirit world, for all the terrible sins he had committed. But poor Raj never even made it out of the Eastern Hemisphere. He mysteriously choked to death on a big fat glob of frozen yogurt at a Baskin-Robbins in Hong Kong. According to Sarah, frozen yogurt—"frogurt"—was his "favorite snack."

His cruel demise wasn't an accident. Obviously not. The leyaks *had gotten to him. I don't believe in accidents. I believe in reasons. It was no accident that Led Zeppelin drummer John Bonham died after eating four ham rolls and drinking forty shots of vodka, was it? John Bonham loved ham rolls and vodka. Likewise, this Balinese heroin dealer hadn't died eating grits or a tuna melt. Neither of these foods would have been fitting. Neither was his "favorite snack."*

On the other hand, the whole story might be a lie. Part of me thinks that Sarah could have made it up in order to justify why the kitchen isn't near the dining room. It isn't even on the same level. A criminal's desperate effort to evade Balinese demons, or at least to keep them off the premises, certainly provides a convenient excuse for the annoying architectural quirks. If every cubic inch of this place were conceived according to the complex laws of Hindu cosmology, then who are we to complain?

Before we arrived, Sarah had described the house she'd picked out as a "brand-new mansion on the ocean." This phrase became a sort of mantra among us. I thought I'd be spending the rest of my life somewhere huge and gaudy, with gold fixtures and marble floors and unused-but-fully-stocked refrigerators—like the houses on MTV's Cribs.

But no: In spite of everything, Sarah's heart is still too pure to be such a creative liar. Plus I know better. I was a religion major. Someone built this house out of fear of a greater supernatural power, and I respect that. Nobody else does. Sarah says she loves the place, but she secured the deal to buy it. Admitting that she hates it would mean admitting to accidentally screwing the rest of us over—me, most of all, because this house was supposed to be my victory and retribution. The others freely complain that it's a big pain in the ass. Madeline outright loathes it. Every day, she rants about the lousy ventilation. But I, for one, am reassured by the building's spiritual fortitude.

Not that leyaks pose any threat to me. They don't waste time tormenting non-Hindus. Yet, where matters of *faith are concerned—anyone's faith—I reserve a degree of respect, even awe. Our residence is probably the only one in all Hispaniola that can boast of being* leyak *free. And so I feel the need to pay tribute to this anonymous Indonesian drug dealer in a personal, sacred way, whether he ever existed or not.*

I know that we're living in his home for a reason. We made our escape. He didn't. Fate left his sanctuary abandoned on a desolate strip of unnamed beachfront road, and through Sarah's wheelings and dealings in the Dominican cash-up-front real estate market, it became our sanctuary. There must be a connection, some mystery involving the intervention of an Unseen Hand. Not that I necessarily want to figure out the particulars. There's a reason you hear an eerie voice proclaim: "Here's to my Sweet Satan" when you play the vinyl of "Stairway to Heaven" backward on a turntable. But nobody understands why. And maybe nobody should. Robert Plant didn't put it there; that's for sure. No way was Robert Plant smart or motivated enough to think of backmasking. This is the same goofball who shouted, "I am a golden god!" from a hotel balcony.

The point is: Investigating the supernatural is a risk that certain people shouldn't take. For all we know, it might bite back.

I glowered at the manuscript. Robert Plant is a goofball? I wondered angrily. What about Gabriel himself? Could any of this possibly be true? Could Sarah have really secured the deal to buy their off-kilter Balinese-drug-dealer getaway house? *Sarah Birnbaum: inept real estate mogul,* I said to myself. Forget it. Well, okay, I could believe the inept part. The only other part I could believe was that their other friends hated it. (Who wouldn't? If it even existed.) I still hadn't learned a thing. Well, I guess I'd learned that Gabriel liked Led Zeppelin, or at least knew some Zeppelin trivia. To his credit, it was a step up from the *Friends* theme song.

I scoured a few pages for any more mention of Sarah or any hint about why they'd run away. But there were no clues. Gabriel felt guilty, and he seemed to think that he'd talked the rest of them into doing something bad. I got that. But what about Sarah? She was mostly absent, as far as I could tell. After the bit about Raj Bhutto, the only name that seemed to pop up with any regularity was their friend Madeline's—and mostly in the context of strange arguments with not-so-subtle sexual overtones. Gabriel was clearly a lot more interested in her than he was in my sister (probably a good thing). Maybe this was what he'd been talking about when he'd told me every single straight male thinks about hooking up with a friend—"maybe once, maybe a thousand times."

I closed my eyes, trying to remember what Madeline looked like. I'd only met her three times before, up at Columbia. I definitely remembered that she was hot: tall and skinny, like a model (but less alien), with long curly brown hair and ivory skin that had obviously never seen a zit and never would. I also remembered thinking that she *knew* she was hot—and she'd probably gotten away with a lot in life because of it, particularly with horny adolescents like me. She was nice enough, but she mostly kept grinning at me as if to say, *It's okay if you're imagining me naked right now. Run with it.*

It was weird, though. The harder I tried to picture her face, the less clear it became. The memory kept fading into a fuzzy jumble of lots of different girls from the past: random childhood friends of Sarah's that she'd lost touch with, Emma's older cousin Nadine, even the cute twentysomething chick who sometimes works the counter at Mr. Aziz's deli. In the end, I could conjure up only a dim, tantalizing image of Petra, smiling sadly and saying, "I'm sorry, Hen. I still have feelings for you. It's just that my band needs a real bass player now. . . . Okay, sweetie?"

CHAPTER FIVE
Getting My Foot in the Door

"Hen! Open up. Come on. Stop giving me the silent treatment. I'm your sister."

I bolted upright in bed. *Jesus.* I rubbed my bleary eyes, disoriented. The doorknob was shaking. Gabriel's manuscript lay open beside me on the rumpled covers. I grabbed it and shoved it under my pillow.

"Uh, one second," I croaked. My throat was dry. I blinked at the clock radio on my bedside table. It was 7:45 P.M. When had I fallen asleep?

"Mom and Dad told me to tell you that they won't start eating until you come down," Sarah said.

I sniffed, catching a faint whiff of Indian takeout. My stomach rumbled. I hadn't eaten anything since the egg sandwich

Mom made me this morning. "Did they order from Taste of Tandoor?" I asked, stumbling out of bed toward the door. I twisted the lock and threw the door open.

Sarah stood before me in a filthy, loose-fitting Columbia sweat suit—her old gardening and exercise clothes. A few wispy strands of black hair hung in her sweaty face. The rest was pulled back in a bun. Her hands were caked with dirt. She'd taken off her shoes, but aside from a pair of pristine white socks, she looked and smelled as if she'd just gotten into a mud fight. My nose wrinkled.

"Mom and Dad want us to start eating as a family," she said.

I blinked at her, both exhausted and wide-awake.

A strange electric current surged through me. If Gabriel's diary *were* true, then I'd been offered a glimpse of Sarah's secret life—something I'd never experienced before, not even before the disappearance. (I'd never stumbled upon any diary *she'd* kept.) For the first time ever, part of me felt as if I truly were staring at a stranger. I resisted the urge to ask her if she'd found any Balinese demons in our backyard or if buying a Dominican beachfront mansion was easier than renting a loft in Chinatown.

"They want us to eat as a family, huh?" I finally said. "Does that mean they want us to eat together? Or do they want us to try to pretend we're just like everyone else?"

She rolled her eyes. "Come on, Hen."

"What have you been doing, anyway?" I asked.

"Trying to tackle the garden," she said, sounding over-whelmed.

"Literally?"

She laughed and shook her head, plodding down the steps. "Just come downstairs, okay? We were getting worried. You've been up here for hours."

"If we're going to start eating as a family, shouldn't you wash up?"

"Since when have you become such a stickler for hygiene?" she shot back. "You must have really matured while I was away."

My jaw tightened. Sarah hadn't earned the right to joke around with me about this past year. Not yet. Until she told me the truth about everything, I couldn't foresee a time when she ever would.

"I want to hear about your bass lesson," she added. "I couldn't get much out of Mom or Dad. But Dad's head is in his taxes."

My veins buzzed. "Did Gabriel call you?"

"Nope. I haven't heard from him all day. He's lying low."

I watched as she disappeared around the corner on the first floor—then I closed my door and dashed back to bed, fumbling for my cell phone. I yanked Gabriel's manuscript out from under the pillow and punched in the number on the plastic cover. After four long rings, there was a click.

"Hello?" a groggy voice answered.

I wasn't sure I recognized him. "Gabriel?"

"Madeline?"

I frowned. "No, this is Hen Birnbaum," I said, deepening my voice. (Telemarketers made the same mistake. I couldn't count the number of times I'd been called ma'am since I'd been old enough to answer the phone—but it outnumbered the times I'd been called sir by about four hundred to one, and it never failed to humiliate. Sarah was wrong: I couldn't have matured *that* much.)

"Oh, hey," he said, sounding amused. "Sorry, I didn't look at the caller ID. I'm a little out of it." He yawned. "I was just taking a nap. What's up?"

"I . . . um—I just wanted to apologize for bolting on you this morning," I stammered.

"Don't worry about it." He chuckled. "I probably would have done the same thing in your shoes."

I held my breath, waiting for him to mention the missing manuscript. Calling him probably wasn't such a great idea. What if he asked how I'd gotten his number? No big deal: I could always tell him that Sarah had given it to me. "I should have at least said good-bye," I told him. "It was rude."

"Well, I appreciate the call, but you don't have to apologize. There isn't exactly an appropriate way to behave given the circumstances, you know? I guess that's why I offered you the Bloody Mary. You didn't tell Sarah about that, did you?"

"No." I wondered if this was a convoluted way of hinting that he knew what I'd done.

"Good. I mean—well, it's cool if you did, too," he said. "You can tell her whatever you want. I'm not in a position to set boundaries or ask for favors." He laughed again. "I'm definitely not in a position to judge abrupt departures."

I chewed my lip. "Well, um . . . thanks. Would it be cool if we rescheduled? I could come back tomorrow."

"You really want to take bass lessons with me?"

"Yeah. I think I do. At least for now."

"Well, that's great," he said. "Tomorrow works. My schedule isn't very booked at the moment. Want to say ten thirty?"

"In the morning?" I asked.

He laughed. "Yeah. I'm not so much of a night owl anymore."

"Okay. That's what I thought you meant. I'll see you then."

The conversation at dinner that night, our first meal together since Sarah's return, revolved entirely around me, and how I should find a summer job in the music industry. I couldn't tell if this was because Mom, Dad, and Sarah had reaffirmed their secret pact to avoid discussing Sarah's disappearance at all costs (maybe while I'd napped?), or because they'd simply given up: Now that she was back, there was no longer any point in trying to pretend we *weren't* lunatics. We should all feel free to act as deranged as we wanted. Life would be easier. It was liberating in a way, and I was too tired to question it.

Sarah recommended that I take the subway up to Columbia to look at something called the Job Board, which was where she'd found the gig at the homeless shelter she'd briefly had last summer. Mom agreed that this was a good idea and offered to pack a lunch tomorrow for the long ride to Morningside Heights. Dad recommended that I talk to Emma's father, as he was an entertainment lawyer with "notable musician clients, or so I've heard." This propelled the evening to even more dizzying heights of absurdity, as Dad had never made any secret of the fact that he disapproved of Mr. Donovan Wood, Esquire—who drank too much, wore flashy suits, and was generally as loud and boorish as Dad was rigid and demented. Plus his "notable clients" were mostly lame emo acts.

I kept quiet, thinking about all the things I could have said. For instance, I could have mentioned that I'd never once expressed any interest whatsoever in working in the music industry. I could have also mentioned that being a musician and working in the music industry were two different things—and in fact largely unrelated—or that many musicians hated music industry types. But to point out the obvious would be to shatter the fragile, beautiful madness we'd established. Best just to play along. It was actually enjoyable—a truly surreal moment, and one worth savoring, as if I were watching a favorite sitcom and then somehow *poof*! I magically stepped through the screen to become a part of it. There were no longer any rules.

"You know, I think you may be onto something with this summer job idea," I said later, as the four of us did the dishes together. "Did you know that every single member of the Beatles interned for a record company? It's how they got their foot in the door. It's part of why they became so famous."

Sarah giggled.

"Is that true?" Mom asked.

"Yes, Mom," I said. "Yes, it is."

Not that I ever needed an excuse to drop by Emma's after dinner, but I was glad to be able to claim the urgent necessity of speaking to Mr. Wood about summer job opportunities—*right away*. He wasn't at home: even better. Ironically, he and Mrs. Wood were at something called the Indie Rock Awards to see one of his has-been emo clients accept a statue for Lifetime Achievement. (For what? Whining?) I flopped down on Emma's bed and rubbed my eyes. Maybe I should just crash here for the night. I'd never spent the night before, but weird times called for weird measures.

"My God, classic," Emma said, after I'd described the dinner conversation in all its twisted glory. "That's one for the *Best of the Birnbaums* holiday DVD. But you know what? Your parents are right."

"About what?"

Emma sat down at her desk and clicked onto the internet. "A job is just the thing to keep you from stewing about Petra and Sarah."

"Stewing?" I glared at her. "*Stewing?*"

"You know what I mean," she said. "You need a full-time distraction. You need a boss to complain about, a Xerox machine that never works, an office floozy to crush on. You need water cooler banter. Routine, Hen. Routine and normalcy." She swiveled around and looked me in the eye. "Speaking of which, please tell me you didn't read that manuscript you stole."

"I didn't," I said.

"You're lying."

I closed my eyes, wishing I were a narcoleptic. The ability to slip instantly into a comatose state suddenly seemed liked the most enviable condition God had ever seen fit to bestow upon humanity. I wondered if there were any pills that would trigger it.

"You're going to give it back first thing tomorrow, right?" she asked.

"Jesus, Emma!"

"Sorry, sorry. I won't nag. I won't ask you to tell me about it, either. You'll tell me when you'll tell me." She turned her attention back to the computer. "Now let's get started on this job hunt. It's a good thing my dad isn't home. Trust me, you don't want to talk to him about this. He'll just hold you back."

I laughed in spite of myself. "From what? Becoming an entertainment lawyer?"

"Come on, Hen. Asking my dad for a favor is like volunteering to have a circus clown throw a pie in your face."

She had a point. Mr. Wood was always cackling—laughter that verged on the mildly horrific, as he had no chin, just a vast, blubbery neck. Whenever he spotted me on the street schlepping my bass somewhere, he flashed the heavy metal horns and shouted "Disco sucks!" Other than that, he preferred not to address me directly. The first time we'd ever met, in fact, he hadn't even said hello. Emma and I were six years old, playing hopscotch in front of our houses. He'd just smirked and asked her, "Who's the skirt?" Yet hardly a day had gone by when part of me hadn't wished *he* were my father instead of my own.

"I'm going to get a job, too," Emma announced out of nowhere.

"You are?"

"If you are, yeah. Solidarity, my friend. Power to the people. As long as you come to this Journey concert with me. It's only three weeks away. The clock is ticking."

"I'll come, I'll come," I groaned.

"Good. Hey, if you want to know the truth, I was planning on getting a summer job anyway."

I sat up straight. "Really?"

"No. But times are tough all over. My parents stopped giving me an allowance. Now I have to beg for money when I need it. You know what Dad said the other night, and not as a joke? 'Using the law to screw people over may be recession proof, but nothing is Depression proof.' He was on his third cocktail." She leaned forward, squinting at the screen and sliding the mouse around. "I think I want to find something in conflict resolution . . ." Her voice trailed off. She'd clicked on a site called referee.com. From across the room, I couldn't see anything other than the logo and a picture of a bald guy in a striped shirt with a whistle in his mouth.

"You want to work for the NBA?" I asked.

"I'm weighing a lot of different options. This is for your benefit, Hen. If you get in a fight with your sister, I want to be there to stop it."

"Yeah, well. Good luck with that." I lay back down again.

Maybe we *did* need a referee. I hadn't had a normal conversation with Sarah since she'd gotten home. It was all bickering and frustrated silences and obtuse hints at huge mysteries. But what had I expected? On other hand, we didn't use to fight. Before she'd disappeared, Sarah and I had always pretty much gotten along. Of course we had: We'd been allies, united against our parents' relentless neurotic onslaught. But now it seemed that they were on the same team, united against *me*.

I sighed, listening to Emma clicking away.

Now that I thought about it, the only time I'd ever gotten into a real, honest-to-God fight with the old Sarah—aside from that babysitting debacle with Emma—was early last summer, when she told me she was worried that I didn't have enough "guy friends." After assuring her that I wasn't gay, I reminded her that if Emma were a guy, I would have had a "guy friend." Emma just happened to be female. And it wasn't like I was an angry loner or anything. I got along fine with "guys" at Franklin—just not to the point where I could show up unannounced at their homes and hog their TV remotes. It had pissed me off that Sarah could be so stupid. She'd just graduated from an Ivy League college. And look where "guy friends" had gotten her: a rat hole in Chinatown.

"Wow," Emma muttered in the silence.

"What?" I said.

"Some of these job sites are really amazing. Did you know that you can earn two hundred bucks an hour as a topless housecleaner, plus tips?"

CHAPTER SIX

$30,000 for a Grilled Cheese Sandwich on eBay

The next day got off to a crappier-than-usual start.

I was exhausted, for one thing. I'd stayed at Emma's until one o'clock in the morning—much later than usual—watching a *Behind the Music* rerun marathon on the VH1 Classic network. (I'll never understand why VH1 temporarily cancelled this show. Best. Cheesy. Melodrama. Ever.) Coincidentally, the theme was forgotten bands from the nineties: Blues Traveler, Barenaked Ladies, and Hootie and the Blowfish (how had *they* sold sixteen million albums?). It culminated with a ninety-minute special about the New Kids on the Block. I wondered if Gabriel had watched, too, seeing as one of the few things I knew for certain about him was that he was in a nineties nostalgia band—whatever that even meant. Then I remembered he didn't have a TV.

Emma and I gave up on the job hunt after it became clear that very few employers were looking to hire sixteen-year-olds with no skills whatsoever. After briefly asking myself whether I should be concerned that Mom and Dad hadn't called to check up on me, I stumbled home and collapsed into bed without bothering to brush my teeth.

That's when the trouble started.

Stupid, stupid dreams.

Four summers ago there had been a curious (and, yes, possibly supernatural) incident between Emma and me. We'd both had dreams about going to school naked, and we both made the mistake of telling each other about them. Or rather I made the mistake of telling *her*, and then she confessed that she'd had the exact same dream a week earlier. The details they shared—exposure of our private parts during assembly, the improvised use of arts-and-crafts smocks to hide our shame, a cameo appearance by both sets of parents—were so eerily similar that we made a pact never to talk about dreams again.

And what do you know? Last night, I dreamed I made out with her.

I admit: It wasn't the first time I'd had a dream like this. But this was the most vivid. I even remembered what she was wearing: a flowery sundress, straight out of *The Great Gatsby*. We were at the Journey concert. (Not that *The Great Gatsby* has anything to do with Journey, but causal relationships aren't big in Dreamworld.) As usual, I awoke with a start just as it was getting intense. Then I tossed and turned for the rest of the night, wondering if Emma had ever had a make-out dream (or more) about *me*. Of course, the lesson I'd learned from the going-to-school-naked dream—and that I hoped Emma had, too—was that stupid, stupid dreams mean nothing. It was the lie I clung to, at any rate.

I will say this: Our pact to shut up about dreams kept me from obsessing about them more than I probably would have.

That's what I reminded myself when I finally staggered out of bed that morning. *Focus on what's real.* Real life was not Emma's lips pressed against my own in the middle of a standing ovation for "Come Sail Away." (Which isn't even a Journey song; it's Styx—More proof that dreams mean nothing.) Real life was Dad doing his taxes at the dining room table. It was Mom frying up another egg sandwich to go for me, Sarah tearing up weeds in the backyard, and Mom and Dad letting her do whatever she wanted even though none of them would offer up a single detail about last year. It was Gabriel's stolen manuscript still hidden under my pillow. Above all, real life was being late for my 10:30 bass lesson and not being at all sure that I wanted to go anymore, anyway.

Gabriel answered the door in an oversize black Tupac, R.I.P. T-shirt and green boxer shorts. He didn't bother to put on pants after I came in. Apparently our relationship had entered a new, much-too-intimate, pantless phase that he hadn't thought to clear with me first. He draped his bass around his neck and shoulders and plugged into his practice amp, then turned to me expectantly.

I stood by the door, my own bass still zipped up in the case on my back.

"What's wrong?" he asked.

"Am I supposed to play in my underwear, too?"

His pale cheeks reddened. "Whoops. I totally forgot to get dressed. I don't get outside as much as I should." He grabbed a pair of jeans from a rumpled laundry pile near his futon and shimmied into them without taking his bass off, nearly tripping and toppling headfirst into the amp.

That pretty much set the tone for the next several minutes. I clumsily plugged my bass into the other input. The speaker immediately began to buzz, an irritating fact both of us chose to ignore. Then, without explanation, he began to play the opening riff to Pearl Jam's "Jeremy." It actually sounded pretty good. I mean, I hate the song, but he nailed the harmonics and even kept a little rhythm track going by plucking a muted string on every second and fourth beat. I had the feeling that he was showing off for me with the one song he'd learned to play well. I admit: I used to do the same thing with "Another One Bites the Dust" when I was in PETRA. After maybe six-dozen repetitions, he encouraged me to try to "sound out the melody." The wrong notes I offered in response were so cringeworthy that they eventually prompted him to ask, "Do you know the song 'Jeremy,' by Pearl Jam?" I told him I didn't.

On the glass-half-full side of the situation, he didn't mention the stolen manuscript. I relaxed enough to convince myself that he still didn't know it was missing. Finally he stopped playing. We stood like that for a while—facing each other in awkward silence, joined by the cords in his amp—until I decided to take a risk.

"So, what are those manuscripts piled up over there by the door?" I asked.

"They're copies of a very long love letter to your sister," Gabriel replied.

I stiffened, accidentally banging my tuning pegs against one of the bare walls. Needless to say, this was not the answer I'd wanted or expected.

He laughed. "Well, not entirely. I mean, I do want to tell my story. Once I know what it is. I'm sending it out to a bunch of publishing houses, actually. I saw on a literary blog that memoirs are really big now—especially memoirs written by criminals. And given how screwed up the world is, I'm thinking that people might actually want to read it, especially since it's one of those tell-alls that's actually true. Plus, it can't hurt that I'm young. So I want to cash in. Once I do, I can pay my debt for my crimes."

I nodded with a sickly smile frozen on my face. I realized now that I was wrong in thinking that my family was certifiable (well, not really). But Gabriel was in a different league. He frightened me. His tone was perfectly neutral, too, so I couldn't tell if he was joking or not. Not that I even understood half of what he was saying.

"You know, I never told Sarah how I felt about her," he added. "Or she never told me about how she felt about *me*—and things got out of control because of it. Plus, I fooled myself into thinking I was in love with this other friend of ours, a girl named Madeline. . . . Well, it's a long story. You'll see. Someday."

"Can I read the manuscript now?" I blurted out.

"No, Hen, I'm sorry. Not until it's finished. That's only the intro, anyway. Just a teaser that will hopefully get a book deal. Sarah can't read it until it's published either. None of us can, because I still don't know how it'll end. Look, I apologize if I'm being inappropriate here, but judging from the way you turned red and ran out yesterday . . . Are you really tight friends with some girl who you have a secret crush on?"

I blinked. *Jesus.* Where had that come from? My lips trembled. I felt an inexplicable urge to confess: that I'd already stolen one of the manuscripts and that my brain was short-circuiting not knowing *why* Sarah and her friends had run away, or why she and Gabriel had inexplicably come back. On the other hand, I didn't want to admit I was a liar and a thief. And I sure as hell didn't want to admit to the dream I'd had about Emma. I couldn't get a grip on *what* I wanted from this guy. Could it be that in some deeply, profoundly, psychologically damaged way . . . I wanted to impress him? Now I *was* frightened. Honestly, who would want to impress this schmuck? Was it because he was so close with Sarah? Or because he seemed to know so much about me, even though he didn't know me at all?

"I don't mean to pry," Gabriel said.

"No, it's just— My best friend is this girl named Emma," I stammered. "But there's nothing between us. I swear. She isn't the love of my life who's been hiding in plain sight all along. See, the thing is, though, my girlfriend dumped me the other night. The night you and Sarah came home."

"I *do* see," Gabriel said. "What's your ex's name?"

"Petra Dostoyevsky. Why?"

"It's just interesting that you referred to Emma by name and Petra Dostoyevsky by label. I'd say that Emma means more to you—and in all ways. It's a sign. It's not the first time you used that line, either, isn't it?"

"What line?"

"The love of your life who's been hiding in plain sight all along," he said. "It sounds rehearsed."

It was. There's a story there. Franklin is a nice, boring, mostly well-adjusted high school, as far as it goes. But it *is* a high school, so there are a few sad troglodytes who believe that the key to popularity is to be an asshole. Since Emma and I pretty much keep to ourselves, people generally let us go about our silly lives. But every now and then someone—usually an athlete, sad but true (even their identities lack imagination)— will ask us what our "deal" is. Sometimes they'll ask if we're "friends with benefits." To which Emma will reply yes: We both come with dental insurance and a $250 deductible.

Mostly, however, they'll accuse us both of being gay. "Are you gay, or what?" (An actual quote, verbatim. Staggering, isn't it?) A long time ago, we came up with a standard response: Drop our jaws, stare at each other as if we've been struck by lightning, and spout a teen movie cliché. "Oh my God, Hen, you're the love of my life, and you've been hiding in plain sight all along!" "Emma, you're the girl next door, and I totally just realized you complete me." "You *are* the cheese to my macaroni." And so forth. It helps. Troglodytes don't like to be confused.

"How about we play 'Smells Like Teen Spirit'?" Gabriel suggested.

Coming here was a terrible idea. I should have stayed at home and read the stolen manuscript. It was all getting a little too heavy, a little too fast. Yesterday, the proverbial arm was numb; now it was raw and exposed, and I didn't know why. But I couldn't bring myself to leave. Gabriel was a deeply messed-up individual, his criminal past notwithstanding— and he was a joke of a bass teacher, my ostensible reason for being here . . . plus he suffered from alcoholism and OCD and who knew what else (at least judging from the maniacal schlock I'd read). But he was wise. Wasn't he? Or maybe not so much wise as intuitive . . . and definitely scary—but less in a sketchy psycho way and more in a $3.95-a-minute psychic hotline way . . . or . . .

"Look, Hen, you can split if you want," he said.

I hesitated, thinking of what he'd written in his diary. "Can I ask you something?"

"Of course," he said.

"Do you believe in the supernatural?"

He smiled. "It depends. Why do you ask?"

"See, Emma and I have this weird history of dreaming the same thing. It freaked us out so much that we made a pact not to talk about it. But then she dreamed that Sarah came home, and the next night Sarah *did* come home. And then last night I dreamed . . ." I didn't finish. I could feel my face getting hot.

For a long time, Gabriel sat very still, staring into space with a glassy-eyed, meditative look. "Sometimes coincidences get the best of you," he said. "Have you heard about the woman who sold an old grilled cheese sandwich on eBay for thirty thousand dollars?"

I frowned. "Is there a punch line coming?"

"No, I'm serious. It had an image of the Virgin Mary burned into it. Think of it this way: I don't believe that Jesus put it there. Do you? On the other hand, I've seen a picture of the sandwich. The burn pattern really *does* look like the Virgin Mary."

"What the hell are you talking about, Gabriel?"

"Just this: If Emma is so in tune with your dream life and your real life, she *has* been hiding in plain sight," he said. "It's not a coincidence, either. I say go for it now, before it gets too late or too weird or too crusty, like an old grilled cheese sandwich. I didn't mean to upset you, though, Hen. I know you're going through a tough time."

I laughed.

"What?" he said.

"I wonder what my parents would say if they could see me right now." I looked down at my feet. "You know—if they could listen in on this conversation."

Gabriel took off his bass and placed it on the stand. "Honestly? I don't think they would mind. Your parents love you, Hen. So does Sarah. I know they do."

I swallowed. "I didn't say they didn't," I said quietly.

"But you think they're insane," he said. "Who isn't, though? Look, Hen, it doesn't matter *what* your parents are. You're closer with them than I ever was with mine. So is Sarah. I know, because Sarah told me how your family works. And no matter how crazy they are, or how much they drive *you* crazy, it's always better to be closer than to be distant. That goes for Emma, too. Believe me, I know from experience."

A small lump mysteriously began to well up in my throat. I blinked a few times, avoiding his eyes. Why was he telling me all this? I hadn't asked to be lectured or psychoanalyzed—and I sure as hell didn't want to hear his opinions about my family's operating procedures. He was wrong, anyway: My parents *were* distant, at least when it came to talking about Sarah. "If Sarah is so close with us, then why did she run away with you?" I asked after a minute. "What made her do it?"

Gabriel shrugged. "To tell you the truth, Hen, I'm still trying to figure that out myself."

CHAPTER SEVEN

A Fist Bump from the Unseen Hand

I never made it to Emma's that day. Something happened after I left Gabriel's apartment—something that made wonder if his freakish brand of mysticism wasn't so far off the mark. Maybe there *is* an Unseen Hand that manipulates all the baffling coincidences in our lives, pushing us toward Enlightenment or smacking us if we try to figure out who recorded the backward Satanic messages on "Stairway to Heaven."

Petra called.

I was about a block from the subway. For the first couple of rings, I stood there on the sidewalk and stared at the caller ID, debating whether or not to answer. I hadn't spoken to her since the night she'd fired me. I wondered what would happen if I told her that Sarah had come home. I wondered if she would care. Finally, curiosity got the best of me.

"Hello?" I answered.

"Hey, Hen? Guess what? Bartholomew Savage got us a show at the Bimbo Lounge!"

Wow. I wondered what had compelled her to share this wonderful news with me, her ex-bassist/boyfriend. The sheer joy of it? That she'd really meant what she said, that we *were* still friends? None of this mattered, though, because it was impossible. For one thing, Bartholomew Savage couldn't get anyone a show anywhere. He was fourteen. Besides, the Bimbo Lounge was one of those trendy Lower East Side bars where indie legends like Iggy Pop and A&R guys from major labels were rumored to hang out. You definitely needed a demo or a reputation to get on their bill, and PETRA had neither.

"No kidding," I said. "How'd he manage that?"

"His older brother is a bartender there," she said breathlessly.

"Really? I had no idea."

"Yeah. He's really a cool guy, too. Victor. I was hanging out at their apartment, and Bartholomew introduced me to him. He told me that they're starting this new thing this summer: Underage Talent Night. The first one is June twenty-fourth. It's a Wednesday. We're gonna be the opening act."

I chewed my lip. Taking this call was a mistake. "Are you putting me on?" I asked.

"No! Look, Hen, I'm calling because I want you to be in the band again." Her voice was still bubbling with excitement.

"You do?"

"Well . . . yeah. I mean, I have to be honest with you, though. I asked George Monroe if he wanted to be in the band, and he said yes."

A smile curled on my lips. I deserved a gold star for being so smart, didn't I? I wondered if they'd made out yet. "So what does that mean? We're going to have two bassists?" I thought of the bass face-off I'd just had with Gabriel. I wished I hadn't. The opening riff to "Jeremy" began to echo in my head in a continuous loop.

"No, he's on vacation with his family in Europe until July Fourth. But here's the deal, Hen. I gave this a lot of thought. If you practice really hard, and we kill this gig, I'll tell George that I've changed my mind. Okay, sweetie?"

"Ah. So this is one of Life's Second Chances."

Petra didn't answer right away. If Emma had been on the phone, she'd have taken the cue: *"Indeed, my friend. Are you man enough to accept the challenge?"* Then again, Emma would never have fired me from a band in the first place.

What Petra eventually said was, "This doesn't mean that we're back together, though. Like as a couple. I just want to be clear. So it doesn't get awkward or anything."

"The thought never crossed my mind," I replied, which was true.

"Hey, Hen, are you all right?"

"Fine. Why?"

"I don't know. You sound sort of weird."

"It's been a weird couple of days," I confessed.

"I know. And I'm sorry I don't want us to be, like, involved anymore, but—"

"No, no. It's not that." I paused. In spite of everything that bugged me about Petra, I knew that if she made a promise, she stuck to it. "Listen . . . if I tell you something, will you swear not to tell anyone?"

"Uh-oh. I don't like the sound of—"

"Yes or no," I interrupted.

"Well . . . okay. Yes."

"Sarah's back," I said. "She came home two nights ago."

"Oh, my *God*," Petra whispered. "Are you serious?"

"Yeah. She won't tell me why she ran away, though. But the good news is that I'm taking bass lessons. So the timing sort of works out perfectly."

There was a pause. "What do you mean?"

"One of Sarah's friends, one of the guys she ran away with, came back, too," I explained. "He's hiding out in the East Village and giving me bass lessons."

"Are you serious?" Petra asked again.

"Yeah. I think I might have even told you about him. His name is Gabriel Stern. He was in a nineties nostalgia band. They were called Friends."

"Oh, my— That's genius!"

My forehead wrinkled. "It is?"

"Yeah, that name!" she exclaimed. "And the whole *concept*! It's such a coincidence! I was thinking that nineties retro was totally our thing, but we never, like, *identified* it. And this whole time, I've been looking for a better word than 'retro.' Or 'tribute.' But that's it. 'Nostalgia.' A nineties nostalgia band. It's so warm and fuzzy. Genius!"

I blinked. Genius? Really? And was nineties nostalgia "totally our thing"? I guess it was, if you chose to drink this freshest batch of Petra's Kool-Aid. Most of our songs *were* rap rock. I'd always described PETRA's sound to Emma as midcareer Beastie Boys—but only when played on their instruments, and with a female singer (minus their talent, too). Petra's excitement scared me. It meant I had even more in common with Gabriel than I'd realized. This was bad.

"Oh, Hen?" she said. "One more thing. I changed our name."

"You did?"

"Yeah. PETRA is too me-me-me. What do you think of Dawson's Freak?"

Hmm. I liked PETRA better. It summed us up perfectly, and in all caps no less. But I didn't say anything. Mostly I marveled at how Petra could ignore the news that Sarah had returned, when until two days ago I'd been "the guy whose sister disappeared" and whose "edgy mystique" had attracted Petra in the first place. Oh, well.

"You don't like it," she said in the silence. "Don't you remember the show?"

"Um, yeah. *Dawson's Creek*, right? It was the one with Katie Holmes when she was our age."

"Yeah. Pre–Tom Cruise. And Michelle Williams, pre–Heath

Ledger. But, listen, I've gotta go. My dad's back in town. Did I tell you I'm staying with him over the summer? He lives in SoHo. Hey, why don't you come over tomorrow night? I've got some new material. I want to get it tight before we rehearse with Bartholomew."

"Um . . . sounds great."

"Cool. I'll text you his address. Bye, sweetie."

I hung up. My bass felt very heavy on my back all of a sudden. The sun was hot. I stepped out of the East Village sidewalk traffic into the shade of a nearby tree to call Emma.

"You're not gonna believe this," she answered.

"You're not gonna believe *this*," I replied.

"What?"

"You first," I said.

"Sarah got me a job at New Beginnings," Emma said. "You know, the homeless shelter where she used to volunteer?"

My eyes narrowed. I *did* know. I just didn't know why Emma would possibly want to work there.

"I'm thinking that I might be able to find some clues," she said, answering my unspoken question. "Maybe she told her colleagues stuff that she didn't tell anyone else. She worked there right up until the day before she disappeared."

"And Sarah is cool with all this?"

"Well, I didn't tell her *that* part. But she was really psyched. She told me I'd make a great social worker. It's a volunteer gig, but even my dad is impressed. He said he'll start giving me an allowance again, so I'll have spending money."

I shook my head. "When did all this happen?"

"Just now. I saw her out my bedroom window, you know, working out back in your garden. I decided to drop by and say hi. She made me promise like a zillion times not to tell anybody that she's home, especially my parents—even though they can see her if they look out *their* window. So what's *your* big news?"

"It's um . . . well, I guess it's just as weird in its own way. Petra asked me to come back to the band. She got us a gig at the Bimbo Lounge."

"You didn't say yes, did you?" Emma asked sharply.

I frowned. "Actually, I did."

"Why?" she demanded.

"What do you mean, why? She needs a bassist."

"Does this mean you're gonna start *shtupping* again?"

I rolled my eyes. "We never *shtupped* in the first place. But, no. She made it clear that we were broken up for good."

"And you really want to play a gig at the Bimbo Lounge?" Emma asked.

"Why wouldn't I?"

"It's a dump, for starters. But that's not what worries me."

Amazing: For the first time in my life, I regretted making the Emma call. "What worries you, Emma? Do tell."

She sighed. "This isn't some big, momentous turning point in your life, Hen. A film crew isn't about to start making the PETRA rockumentary."

I laughed. "How can you be so sure? By the way, we're not called PETRA anymore."

"You're not?"

"No. Now we're Dawson's Freak. We're a nineties nostalgia act. Not tribute. Not retro. *Nostalgia.* Just like Gabriel's old band, Friends." I almost giggled.

"Does that mean you're going to start wearing wool caps and beepers and flannel shirts?" she asked with a big glob of fake sweetness.

My face soured. "Why are so you pissed about this?" I asked.

"I'm not. I'm disappointed," she said.

"Jesus, Emma! You sound like my dad."

She sniffed. "I'm glad I do. You're setting yourself up to get hurt at a really weird time in your life. You should know better. I would say Petra should, too—but she's too wrapped up in Petra."

"The person or the band?"

"Whatever," she groaned. "Maybe being back in the band is just the distraction you need. Chances are, you'll never find a job, anyway. I'm not gonna worry about it."

"That's kind of you," I said flatly.

"I should go. I need to bone up on my social work skills. I start tomorrow." Her voice brightened. "Wish me luck!"

"Good—"

Click. She hung up without saying good-bye.

I shoved the phone in my front pocket, feeling out of sorts. Were Emma and I in a fight? I was half tempted to call her back, but thought better of it.

All of a sudden I noticed a sign taped to the tree trunk next to me.

DOG WALKER NEEDED!

What do you know: a job. Just like that. Out of nowhere. The Unseen Hand, fist bumping me! At the very moment I needed it most. And I loved dogs. Woof, woof. I tore the paper off the trunk and shoved it in my back pocket without bothering to read the rest.

I hurried toward the subway, suddenly feeling much better. Dog walking. That was funny. It was better than funny. It was the opposite of "getting my foot in the door" anywhere (except maybe veterinary school). Best of all, it was good material—a nice tidbit for the rockumentary that a film crew *would* make someday, the one that would prove Emma and every other person in my life wrong about everything. I could already picture the trivia spot on the VH1 Classic network:

Before Hen Birnbaum became a world-famous bassist, he was . . .
    A) A referee
    B) A topless house cleaner
    C) A dog walker
We'll be back with the answer, right after this commercial break!

* * *

That night I read the rest of Gabriel Stern's *Diary of My Life on the Lam* cover to cover. It took me about an hour—an hour of my life that I'll never get back. If this was a "very long love letter" to my sister, then Gabriel Stern and I had a very different idea of what a love letter was. I honestly felt sorry for him. It was clearer than ever that he needed the kind of help only institutionalization could provide.

He was right, though: The manuscript didn't have an ending. None of his meandering gibberish, not a single word, had anything to do with the crime they'd committed. I still wasn't any closer to figuring out *why* they'd ended up stuck together in a house haunted by Balinese demons.

Here's an illustrative excerpt—which stuck in my mind only because February 25 happens to be my birthday:

February 25
Today Madeline ran amok and destroyed the living room.
    When we first arrived, the living room was completely barren. Then Sarah bought two huge mirrors and mounted them on opposite walls, facing each other. She said she wanted to make up for the lack of windows by creating the illusion of space. And I have to hand it to her, it really worked. The optical effect was the same as in a barbershop: you would see a line of mirrors, front and back, stretching into infinity.
    But today Madeline snapped. Cool, dry, detached Madeline . . . she tore the mirrors off the walls, shattering

the glass and leaving hideous gashes in the plaster. "How's that for Second Empire?" she shrieked. Then she bolted from the house.

I got nervous. I'm still nervous. "How's that for Second Empire?" What the hell is that supposed to mean?

Sarah sobbed uncontrollably for hours. She kept saying over and over, "Madeline should pay." She gestured hopelessly at the shards of broken mirror on the floor. "She should pay for something."

As it turned out, she did. Six hours later Madeline returned with a huge bronze sculpture that looked like a giant dog turd. She wheeled it into the living room on a dolly. Apparently, she paid 52,000 pesos for it—roughly $4,000. She claimed that a famous Dominican artist had made it and that it was supposed to represent Jean-Paul Sartre's head.

I learned an important lesson from all this. Madeline is to be left alone. None of us have mentioned the incident since it happened, and I don't see any of us speaking up soon. As far as I know, she won't pay for any repairs, either. No, with one violent outburst, she brilliantly established her isolation from the rest of the group. The five of us are not a family, and we never will be. Don't imagine that you're close to me. That's what Jean-Paul Sartre's head reminds us—in the same way a huge missile silo in the middle of nowhere reminds passersby of the potential for nuclear holocaust.

It bears mentioning that Madeline has been acting strange lately. She recently took a cue from Sarah's past and began volunteering as a nurse's aide at the Karl Funkhausen Free Clinic in Puerto Plata. She works in the pediatric oncology unit. Maybe it's the act of caring for terminally ill children that keeps her so beautiful— inexplicably and perfectly preserved, while the rest of us slowly begin to wither. Either that or the sex. She claims she's only working at the clinic to meet Dominican doctors. Whatever the reason, her skin still glows. She still wears her brown curls past her shoulders.

I suppose it also bears mentioning that Karl Funkhausen, Madeline's boss, is our only neighbor. He lives about a hundred yards away in a gorgeous, sensibly built mansion that is probably full of leyaks. He is eighty-four years old.

At fifteen, he was a troop leader in the Hitler Youth. At twenty-five, he was an officer in the Stasi, the East German secret police. At fifty-three, he stole a large amount of Nazi war treasure from the East Germans; sold it on the black market; and moved here, where he founded the eponymous Karl Funkhausen Free Clinic.

He is also very good in bed.

Or so I've heard. Madeline shared this information with everyone seventeen weeks ago. Since then, she and Karl have hooked up on a regular basis, often in her room. I know, because I can always hear her quite clearly through the vent next to my bed, screaming, "Oh my God! Oh my God! Oh my God . . ."

Whenever this happens, I lean close to the vent, take a deep breath, and shout at the top of my lungs "Blasphemy is a sin, too, you know!"

Most of the diary was like this. Right up until the final entry.

About the final entry . . . well, I'm still not sure what it really means. All I know is that it made me sadder and more confused than I was before, and I even laughed and cried a little at the same time, which I never do. It proved that my parents hid even more from me than I'd previously suspected. It showed me that Sarah really was a stranger.

Most of all, it taught me that what I've always taken for granted about my family—that however screwed up we may be, however many secrets we may keep, at least we don't lie to each other—isn't true.

But there's no point in trying to describe it. It's one of those things you have to read for yourself.

May 19
Sarah got another letter today. She's the only one of us who receives mail on a regular basis. Her parents write her once a week.

This time the Birnbaums sent pictures. Sarah showed them to me just now in the living room. I had a hard time focusing because she smelled so bad. She was wearing her gardening clothes. She puts on that same noxious outfit every afternoon. Everything is covered in filth: her boots, her Columbia sweat suit, even her sunglasses. Then again, Sarah has every right to stink. Thanks to her, our back-yard is a colorful wonderland, like a spread from House & Garden. *She proclaimed herself a vegetarian farmer upon our arrival, in honor of the little brother she'll never see again. The garden is another one of her fantasies come true.*

The first picture Sarah showed me was of the five of us.

I remember the night it was taken very clearly. It was about three weeks before graduation, still long before we had any clear notion of the awful step we were about to take. The Birnbaums took us out for a fancy meal, along with Henry. We were all dressed formally, sitting around a candlelit table at Caffè Pertutti on Broadway and West 112th Street, two blocks from campus—arms around each other, smiling broadly.

We all looked so skinny.

Sarah's mother didn't have a head, though. A neat square was cut out directly above her evening dress.

"Why is your mom's head cut out?" I asked her.

"She's crazier now than ever. She hates the way she looks in pictures. She thinks her face will ruin them. But look at Hen. Doesn't he look cute?"

I found it a little uncomfortable to comment on

whether I find Sarah's brother "cute," so I didn't answer. The rest of the pictures were all candid shots of Sarah's parents and her brother, scolding him the way I imagine they once scolded her. In one, Mrs. Birnbaum jabs a chicken leg at him, as if to say, *What kind of person doesn't eat chicken?* I can only guess what her expression is, though, because her head is missing.

"I should really go back to Brooklyn," Sarah told me when we were done.

Poor Sarah, I thought for the 487th time.

She always has this same homesick reaction whenever she gets a letter from home. Every one is filled with hysterical pleas for her to surrender herself to the authorities. The way Mr. and Mrs. Birnbaum see it, if Sarah turns herself in, then Henry can finally learn the truth about why she did what she did. According to Sarah, they still refuse to tell him. They want Henry to hear it from her first. But does Sarah even know why herself? Lord knows, I still can't figure it out. She refuses to admit that I'm completely responsible for it.

The worst Sarah suffered over this was when her parents snuck down to visit back in March. I still can't believe they actually came here.

Mr. and Mrs. Birnbaum donned ludicrous wigs the moment they cleared customs. They didn't want to be recognized. Sarah later told me that they even made up some silly lie for Henry about attending a conference somewhere in Florida. They assumed they were in great *danger, which I still don't understand. Their passports had been stamped. Immigration officials knew they were in the country. They'd already blown their cover. Yet they insisted on disguising themselves like bad hair-transplant models. And if they were so nervous, why did they come in the first place? Madeline's parents don't know where we are, nor do Tony's, nor Rich's, nor above all my dad. None of them want anything to do with us anymore. Wasn't that the whole point, in a way?*

Mr. and Mrs. Birnbaum wouldn't step foot in the house, though. Not that I can blame them for that. Instead, they stayed at the Eurotel, a tacky complex of beachside resorts about four kilometers from the airport. Everyone who works there speaks English or German. Sarah says it's "just like the Catskills." Even its restaurant—"America Restaurant"—features a pianist who knows show tunes.

Dinner that night qualified as one of the oddest experiences in the short twenty-two years of my life. The Birnbaums wouldn't take their wigs off. I hadn't realized just how insane they were before, not even when they'd taken us out to dinner at Columbia. I hadn't realized people like that actually existed. They were a very, very dark comedy come to life.

INT—AMERICA RESTAURANT—NIGHT
MR. BIRNBAUM: Sarah, are you sure you don't want to see my electronic nose hair clipper? I bought it at the

duty-free shop for only four dollars.

MRS. BIRNBAUM: *Irv, you haven't seen your daughter in nine months and you're talking about your nose hair clipper? It's her birthday.*

MR. BIRNBAUM: *What? At least they sell cheap merchandise down here. You know how much this costs in the States?*

MRS. BIRNBAUM: *Stop, already. Sarah, look at you, honey . . . you're so thin. All you eat are these bean sprouts.*

SARAH: *I eat other things, Mom. Tonight I had some squash.*

MRS. BIRNBAUM: *(Weeping suddenly) Why don't you come home with us? Please? Hen misses you! If he knew the truth, that you live like a criminal—*

SARAH: *I am a criminal.*

MR. BIRNBAUM: *Hey! Don't talk back to your mother!*

MRS. BIRNBAUM: *You all used to be such nice kids. Gabriel, what does your father have to say about this? Does he cry himself to sleep every night?*

SARAH: Leave him alone, Mom.

MR. BIRNBAUM: What, he can't speak for himself?

MRS. BIRNBAUM: Can't you just turn yourselves in? Finally? Please?

SARAH: We'll go to jail, Mom, remember?

MRS. BIRNBAUM: But why did you do it, Sarah? Just tell us that much. Was it . . . was it crack? I read somewhere crack is making a comeback.

SARAH: Yes, Mom. We're all on crack.

MR. BIRNBAUM: Of course it wasn't crack, Rachel. Inner-city blacks smoke crack.

SARAH: Inner-city what? Jesus, Dad! Listen to you! You sound like the Ku Klux Klan.

MR. BIRNBAUM: Whatever—African Americans, Afro Americans . . . I can't keep up with your lingo. The disenfranchised, is what I mean.

SARAH: Dad, the president of the United States is an "inner-city black." You went to college in the seventies, for

God's sake! The Cultural Revolution was already over.

MRS. BIRNBAUM: (Sniffing and adjusting her wig) Leave your father alone. He went to a community college, not a big-shot Ivy League school like you. What does a community college know from a "Cultural Revolution"?

MR. BIRNBAUM: Please, let's not fight.

SARAH: Fine. I have to go, anyway. I told Madeline I'd meet her at Karl's.

MR. BIRNBAUM: This Nazi you told us about? (He looks toward the ceiling) Lord God, where did we go wrong?

SARAH: He's not a Nazi. He runs a free clinic.

MRS. BIRNBAUM: You told us he was in the Hitlerjugend.

SARAH: Well, he's sorry, okay?

MR. BIRNBAUM: Sorry? Sorry? What—are you a Catholic now? Ten Hail Marys absolves the murder of six million Jews?

SARAH: He didn't murder any Jews! Just go home! Back to your "inner-city blacks"! Leave me alone! (She bolts from the table)

MR. BIRNBAUM: (Screaming after her) Fine! But before we leave, just tell me what a geriatric Nazi wants with young girls like you! Is he some kind of sick pervert? Is this part of your Cultural Revolution? Just answer me that!

The episode taught me something important. It taught me that our situation is permanent. I knew it all along, but I guess I didn't fully grasp what it meant until I found myself stranded alone with the Birnbaums that night. There's no going back in time, no way to undo what we've done. And sitting there in silence, staring at those wigs and silently cursing Sarah for running off, I saw that my life would never change. This was the closest I would ever come to a family dinner or an evening out on the town. It's hard to believe that a future in the Dominican Republic once seemed so seductive. Not even. In a fateful wrongheaded moment last summer, it seemed like the only viable option I had.

I have to get out of here.

Correction: I have to get Sarah and Madeline and Rich and Tony out of here. It was never their problem. It was always mine. They just made it their own. I have to ante up for them, Sarah most of all. Her pictures clinched it.

PART II

The Gig That Didn't Change Everything

CHAPTER EIGHT
My Glorious Future

Emma stopped by the next morning on her way to her new job. I was still in bed. She'd actually dressed for work. Well, not formally or anything—she *was* going to volunteer at a homeless shelter—but the jeans were new and she'd put her hair in pigtails. She stood in the doorway, smirking as if she had a secret, while I scrambled for the pair of corduroys and T-shirt lying on the floor. I decided it was going to be one of those wear-what-I-wore-yesterday days. I foresaw a lot of those days in the near future.

"I have something for you," she said. "Consider it an apology for hanging up on you yesterday." She reached into her knapsack and handed me a CD.

I was still annoyed with her, or I wanted to be, but I couldn't help but smile. The case was labeled *Hen Birnbaum's Super-Awesome 90s Nostalgia Mix!!!* in felt-tip pen. She'd dotted all the i's and exclamation points with hearts. The song list looked as if it was taken directly from some terrible mail-order compilation CD ("Not available in any store! To use credit card, call . . ."). "The Love Theme from *Titanic,*" by Celine Dion kicked it off. It got progressively more awful from there, with bands and songs I'd barely heard of: "I'm Too Sexy," by Right Said Fred, "Mo' Murda," by Bone Thugs-n-Harmony . . . For some reason, little stars were drawn next to "The Macarena" and Will Smith's "Gettin' Jiggy Wit It." There were also a couple of selections meant as jabs: "Cowboy" and "Devil Without a Cause" by Kid Rock. I'd once made the mistake of telling Emma that I liked Kid Rock, which prompted her to make the universal sign for barfing. By including his songs in this mix, she was reminding me that I had no taste; every song was of equal merit.

"I also left a couple of apologies on your phone," she said. "I think I might have clogged your voice mail."

"Thanks, Emma," I said. I placed the CD on top of my bureau, right beside the joke of a stereo I owned. "But isn't that *Titanic* song called 'My Heart Will Go On'?"

"Yeah, but that's not the song I put on there. It's the actual soundtrack score when Leonardo DiCaprio starts making out with Kate Winslet—you know, on the deck of the ship. No lyrics."

I peered at the case. "Why are some of the songs starred?"

"Those are the ones you've danced to in public," she said.

An embarrassing memory flashed through my mind: trying to teach Emma the dance moves to the macarena last Christmas break in the basement of some senior's brownstone, one of the few big Franklin blowouts we'd talked ourselves into attending.

"How long did it take you to make this?" I asked.

"Not very," she said. "I did it in my dad's office last night. Now, remember, when you listen to this mix thirty years from now, you'll have a perfect little snapshot of this crucial moment in your life. Scientific studies prove that music is a great stimulus for triggering memories. It's true; I saw a documentary about the brain on PBS. It's the second-best stimulus, in fact— right behind odors." She tapped her chin absently. "I tried to capture my own breath in a Snapple bottle, but it was harder than I thought."

"I thought you said that this *wasn't* a crucial moment in my life," I reminded her.

"I'm not talking about being in Petra's band," she groaned. "I'm hoping you'll come to your senses about that sooner or later. I mean, if you're doing it to keep your mind off Sarah, I can understand . . ."

Emma kept talking, but I didn't hear a word after that.

Instead, I heard: *"That morning, Henry 'Hen' Birnbaum's head was in an understandably dark place. He was back in the band, but solving the mystery of his older sister's disappearance weighed on him more heavily than ever. He found himself faced with two pressing questions. Would he return his bass teacher's stolen manuscript? And if so, would he do it in secret?"* (Dramatic pause) *"When he was thirteen, Hen read the unauthorized children's biography of Kurt Cobain*: Kurt Cobain (They Died Too Young). *Cobain was no stranger to petty theft. . . ."*

The man speaking was Jim Forbes, the narrator of *Behind the Music*. At some point yesterday, without warning, he had popped into my head to provide moving commentary on my life. I couldn't get rid of him. Last night at dinner, in fact, his soulful drone allowed me to completely block out whatever Sarah and my parents were blabbering about. (Which brand of mulch was best for the garden? Something like that.) But I didn't mind. I figured it was natural, given the hours I'd spent watching *Behind the Music* reruns—coupled with the newfound certainty, thanks to Emma, that every vital moment of my existence would someday be chronicled in documentary form.

It was all very clear now.

Yes. If everybody else in my life could inhabit a fantasy world that they somehow willed into reality, then I could, too. I *would* be a professional musician. Just like Dad wanted. More important, I would be a rock star. Duh. Of *course* I would be a rock star. And being a rock star would dazzle my family so much that they would spill the beans about Sarah's absence and return, because people always tend to lose their inhibitions and act stupid around famous people. It's a fact. Best of all, this horrible secret that they couldn't share with me, that Gabriel couldn't even *write* about—whatever it was—would seem laughably trivial by comparison. We'd all be a lot happier, and

I'd buy them all yachts.

Seriously: How could the future turn out differently? I was back in the band, and Dawson's Freak would be huge. I knew it. Even the stupid name was growing on me.

True, none of this was terribly original. Half the kids at Franklin wanted to be rock stars (all right, an overstatement). But I wasn't worried. Their bands sucked. And their strategy was wrong. They played the same crappy clubs for the same dozen friends over and over—until even their own band members stopped showing up.

I was too smart to go that route. Having steeped myself in *Behind the Music* lore, I'd learned *the* two crucial lessons.

One: You needed a "thing." And Dawson's Freak had one. We were the world's premier nineties nostalgia band. Grunge, rap rock, "The Love Theme from *Titanic*"—you name it, we would play it. Two: You needed a connection. We had one of those, too: Emma's father. (He even represented Nada Surf, one of *the* big bands of the nineties.) For most of my life I'd known how Mr. Wood made a living, obviously—but only now did I recognize it as the springboard that would catapult me into the stratosphere.

It was wonderful, really. One day, I was a loser—confounded by secrets, with a batty family in danger of sending me over the edge—the next, I was a player, on my way to immortality. Sure, Dawson's Freak had a couple of potential weaknesses. We *were* another power trio, one of maybe five hundred in New York City. Emma, in a bad mood, had once called PETRA "a bad Luscious Jackson rip-off, two decades too late." But now that was a selling point. Plus, we weren't nearly as annoying as Luscious Jackson. Petra was hotter than any one of their now-grizzled members. Sounding like them could only *help*.

Potential problem number two: I was a below-average bassist. Gabriel's lessons certainly wouldn't help matters. They might even hurt. I could hold down the roots of the chords, and I had decent rhythm, but I didn't have an ounce of flair. Every note was a Herculean task to get just right. Then again, Krist Novoselic of Nirvana didn't have a lot of flair, either. And his best friend's dad probably wasn't an entertainment lawyer.

The other pieces were in place. There was our drummer, for starters. Bartholomew Savage looked like a young Justin Timberlake and played like John Bonham himself. He was also a computer whiz who boasted more homemade beats and clever mash ups than Dr. Dre. Plus, the ladies loved him. I'm talking older ladies. The one time we'd performed live, at a Franklin assembly, untouchable junior and senior hotties had checked him out (while ignoring me). But sex appeal was a bonus; with a name like Bartholomew Savage, he was destined to be famous, anyway.

And for a not-so-great guitarist, Petra *was* an incredible stage presence. Her songs were undeniably catchy, too. My favorite was her ode to the STEAL YOUR PARENTS' MONEY stickers, called "Ask Me Why I Stole It."

You want a real answer? I stole it on a whim.
I stole it for the sexy man who always calls me "Slim."
I stole it for the children, for the helpless, for the poor,

I stole it for the crazy lady drinking gin next door.
I stole it for my country, for the people white and black,
I stole it for my parents, cuz I'm gonna give it back.

Petra half sang, half rapped the lyrics, her usual MO. The riff was pretty much indistinguishable from Rage Against the Machine's "Freedom"—but the tempo was slower and funkier and there was more wah-wah. It had a deeper groove, a real power to shake your booty. It would be our hit. All we had to do was record it and pass it along to Emma's father. Then we would get signed. I figured the whole process would take about a month. (It didn't take Fiona Apple much longer than that to get signed after a producer heard *her* demo; it's true, you can watch the *Behind the Music* episode.) We'd definitely be signed before school started in the fall. Given the rigorous demands of recording our first album and placing "Ask Me Why I Stole It" in a Nike or Lexus commercial, I'd have to drop out no later than Christmas break.

And after that . . . well, the next forty years would be a string of delicious clichés. World tours and Wal-Mart in-stores. The record for most iTunes downloads. Drug busts in Japan. Meetings with the Dalai Lama. Guest voiceovers on *The Simpsons*. Orgies at the Plaza Hotel. Séances on Loch Ness. A brief stay at the Betty Ford clinic, followed by plastic surgery—whereupon I would emerge fit as a personal trainer, after I'd drunk four bottles of whiskey a day and snorted up 5.02 percent of Bolivia's total cocaine export. (On second thought, maybe I'd skip the drug phase. I'd have a sex addiction instead.) And, yes, later: the bitter breakup, the solo projects, the years of seclusion . . . then the reunion—a comeback worth zillions and capped off in 2036 by a tearful induction ceremony at the Rock and Roll Hall of Fame.

Oh, and somewhere in there, Petra and I would get married and divorced twice and still be the best of friends. By which point I wouldn't even *care* why Sarah had run away. It would all be long forgotten, and she'd be a quiet, gray-haired shrew, tending the five-acre topiary garden I'd purchased for her on the outskirts of Paris.

In the end, I would be to nineties nostalgia bass playing what Keith Richards is to classic rock guitar. (Laugh all you want now, but watch me in an American Express Card ad campaign coming soon.) I remembered seeing Keith on an HBO special a few years back, jovial and swarthy—smiling as he played all of "Tumbling Dice" a half-step flat. Emma had been with me. She'd started cracking up, her hands mashed against her ears. The sound was so sour, so preposterous, that even the most die-hard Stones fans in the televised audience gazed at each other in disbelief, their faces shriveled like prunes. But Keith kept right on grinning. He jerked and danced and postured. Did he know how terrible he sounded? Did he care? Did it matter? No. Another fifty thousand worshippers would pack the stadium the next night, regardless of how he played. He was beyond criticism: a god.

And that would be me.

Somehow, it made standing there while Emma lectured me

about how stupid I was for rejoining Petra's band all the more poignant.

"As it turned out, Hen didn't have to worry about confessing to the crime of the stolen manuscript," Jim Forbes said. *"The FBI appeared that very day to haul Gabriel Stern away in chains. Hen was no stranger to lucky breaks. The soon-to-be legendary bassist was happy to bid both the lessons and teacher farewell. Years later, when Dawson's Freak broke Michael Jackson's record for most sales of a single album—"*

"Hen!" Emma barked.

"What?"

"Are you even listening to me?"

I swallowed. I could feel myself blushing. "What?" I said again lamely.

"Never mind. Jeez." She rolled her eyes and turned her back on me, then stomped down the stairs. "Oh, and by the way? You're welcome."

So, okay: The FBI didn't appear to haul Gabriel away in chains that day. He called me at around 10:30 to apologize for the half-assed bass lesson yesterday. He also said he had a plan now. Actually, the word he used was "curriculum." When I laughed, he did, too—but, as always, I couldn't tell if he were joking or not because his tone was unreadable. He'd snuck out and purchased a laptop so he could download songs we could both play along to. We could even download bass instruction videos if we wanted.

"We'll break the lesson down into segments," he told me. "Fifteen minutes of warm-up and scales, fifteen minutes of free-form jamming . . . that sort of thing."

I made the mistake of telling him that I could use the structure. Because, yes, I, too, was in a nineties nostalgia band—and our first real gig was at the end of the month.

"No way!" he shouted so loudly that I winced.

I sort of had the feeling he was going a little stir-crazy. It was hard to get him off the phone. He took the news of my gig as a cue to start rambling on and on about the dive bar gigs *he'd* had at Columbia. (They were all catastrophes, attended by no one but Sarah.) I stood at my bedroom window, staring down at Sarah in the garden, debating whether or not to surreptitiously spit on her or yell, "Wash your clothes! You stink!"

Finally at about 10:45, I cleared my throat.

"Hey, Gabriel, I should probably go," I said. "I told my parents I'd look for a job." It wasn't entirely true, but it wasn't an outright lie, either.

"Sure, man—sorry, I'll let you get off," he said. "But, hey, that's so cool about your band and the gig at Bimbo! It's huge. Congratulations."

"Thanks." My eyes wandered over to the rumpled pillow on my bed and the manuscript hidden beneath. I decided to take another risk. "So, do you think you could make it? To the gig?"

"It depends. I'd love to, obviously. I just don't know if it's such a great idea. I nearly had a heart attack buying the laptop, and I was only out and about for less than two hours. But . . . ah, hopefully everything that needs to be cleared up will be cleared up by then and I can start hanging out in public again. Well, either that or I'll be going to jail." He laughed nervously.

"You really think that'll happen?" I asked.

"I'm not sure. But if it does . . . it does."

I chewed my lip. "Well, best-case scenario, if you can make it, do you think you can invite some of your college friends? I'd love to pack the place. Like the guys from your old band and your friend Madeline?"

He chuckled. "Why? Did Sarah say they were in town?"

"Um, no," I said anxiously.

"Sarah is planning to go, though, right? That's one audience member, right there."

"To tell you the truth, I haven't told her about the gig yet."

"Oh." Gabriel took a deep breath. "Well, last I heard, Rich and Tony were on their way to California, and Madeline is still . . . down south. But if Sarah knows something I don't, maybe they can make it."

Neither of us spoke for a moment. My heart beat a little faster.

"Talk to Sarah," Gabriel said finally. "I'll see you tomorrow at 10:30, okay?"

"Okay. See you then."

I hung up. My fingers were clammy. I couldn't tell what was stressing me out more: Gabriel's stolen manuscript or the trillion-ton elephant in the room I had to ignore whenever I talked to him or my sister.

I turned back to the window, watching Sarah as she methodically emptied a plastic sack of fresh soil onto a patch of dirt at the edge of the flagstones. What the hell was even running through her mind right now?

I suppose I *could* talk to her. But I had no idea what I'd say. There had to be a way in—a topic of conversation or line of questioning that would trick her into slipping up about the past year. All I need was one little detail that would allow all the other pieces to fall into place. The problem was, none of the pieces fit. I didn't even know if I *had* any pieces. Could I ask her if Gabriel had somehow talked her into coming back home from the Dominican Republic, to try to reenter society again? That seemed to be the gist of his final diary entry. But, no, there was no way she'd tell me that. Maybe if I posed it as a simple yes-or-no question . . .

I flopped down on my bed, feeling antsy. Could I try to trick Mom or Dad into giving me a clue? Did they even have any? Did anybody really know a goddamn thing? Judging from Gabriel's manuscript, Sarah seemed to be just as clueless about her own disappearance as I was.

Maybe I should forget about the big mystery and focus on what was important: the gig at the Bimbo Lounge. Yes. I should probably even use this vital time alone to practice a little on my own. But to tell you the truth, I hated practicing. It hurt my fingers.

CHAPTER NINE
"Oedipus Wrecks" and Other Hits

Nobody was home when I showed up at Petra's dad's loft that night to work on her new material. Instead I found a note taped to the steel door at the top of a long, rickety wooden stairwell.

Hi, Sweetie,

I tried to leave a message for you but your voice mail is full. You gotta clean out that mailbox, yo! I really shouldn't say "yo," should I? ☺ Anyway, I had to run out to buy batteries for my effects pedals. The door's open. Come in and make yourself at home. Oh, and if you're reading this and you aren't Hen Birnbaum, I've rigged the pipes overhead to release an odorless nerve agent starting . . . NOW. If I were

you, I'd exit the premises immediately. I'm surprised you're
still able to stand. Brain damage can be permanent or
fatal. The worst part is the uncontrollable flatulence. Bye!
xoxo
Petra

Ah, Petra. Did I miss going out with you?

I couldn't even tell. Like I said: funnier in writing.

I pushed the door open and tiptoed inside. I'd never been here before. Petra's dad was a relatively well-known photographer and was always traveling for work. (Her mom, who couldn't take "the rock star lifestyle"—Petra's words—had divorced him and married a chiropractor when Petra was four.) The place was nice. Well, maybe "nice" is the wrong word. It was huge, anyway—one vast room filled with junky antique furniture and big plants. It reminded me of a secondhand shop. All the couches were draped with worn velvet blankets, sun bleached from the massive windows overlooking Broadway. I could tell that Mr. Dostoyevsky thought highly of himself. The walls were lined with dozens of head shots (ones he had taken, I hoped): Ethan Hawke, Janeane Garofalo, and a bunch of other fortysomething actors—weirdly appropriate, given our nineties thing. I'd been a little worried, because from the outside the building didn't look so great. It was a renovated meat warehouse. All the other units were sweatshops.

"Hen Birnbaum felt a twinge of envy staring at those famous

114

faces on the wall," Jim Forbes remarked. *"But even then, he knew his own superstardom would soon dwarf Ethan Hawke's. In December—after their debut album,* Dawson's Freak Show, *went platinum—Petra Dostoyevsky's father quit his day job to become the band's full-time photographer. Later, when he abandoned the rock star lifestyle, he also moonlighted as a babysitter for the eight children Hen and Petra adopted from war-torn Sudan."*

I propped my bass case against a wall and sat down on the couch. Something crumpled in my back pocket—the sign I'd torn off the tree in the East Village yesterday. Ha! Good thing I hadn't changed my pants. I fished it out and unfolded it.

DOG WALKER NEEDED!
For two old English bulldogs and a Labrador
Two families, one building
180 Thomas Street. (Btwn West B'way and Hudson)
You must: love dogs, love *these* dogs,
feed them (3X daily: 9 a.m., noon, 5 p.m.),
bathe and exercise them at the Warren Street Dog Run
$30.00 cash/day—Mon-Fri

Wow. A hundred fifty bucks a week, just for walking three dogs? Not only that; I could hang out in a fabulous Tribeca apartment. *Two* apartments.

I could see it now: One of the families would own a Steinway grand. The five weeks of piano lessons Mom had forced me to take when I was nine years old would finally pay off. I would compose the band's sensitive-but-not-cheesy ballad (a nineties take on the Beatles' "Let It Be") while a couple of purebred old English bulldogs lay at my feet, whatever old English bulldogs were. Better yet, I would confront my fears. Instead of denying the psychic significance of how Emma and I sometimes dreamed the same things at the same time, the lyrics would celebrate it. I'd call it "Dreams Are My Nerve Agent." Perfect.

Once again, I was feeling great.

At the bottom of the page, there was a number, an email address, and a contact name: Glenda Abrahmson. With a name like that, she *definitely* owned a Steinway grand. I yanked my cell phone out of my pocket and dialed her up.

"Hello?" a woman answered. She had an English accent. Her voice was husky.

"Hi, is Mrs. Abrahmson there, please?"

"Speaking," she said. "Who's that?"

"Oh, hi . . . uh—my name is Henry Birnbaum," I said. All at once, I was nervous. "I'm calling about the dog-walking job."

"Oh, terrif!" she exclaimed. "Are you a student?"

Terrif? I relaxed a little. "Actually, I'm on summer break."

"How nice."

"Thank you."

"Have you ever walked dogs before?" she asked.

"Yes," I lied.

"What kind?"

"Two German shepherds." I wanted to sound impressive. Mom and Dad had never let us own a dog, citing allergies I still wasn't sure actually existed.

"I trust this isn't a case of résumé padding," she said drily.

There was a beep. Another call was coming in on my line, from a private number.

"I'm sorry, can you hold on a second?" I asked.

"Go ahead and take it," she said. "I'll see you Monday morning, half past eight. You know where I live, right?"

My eyes widened. That was it? "Uh, yeah," I said uncertainly. "Thanks."

"Thank *you*, Henry Birnbaum," she replied, then hung up.

I pressed the flash button, hoping it was Emma. I couldn't wait to prove to her how everything in my life was suddenly falling into place. "Hello?"

"Hen, do you know where Sarah is?"

It was Dad. Ever since he'd become convinced the government was spying on us, he'd kept our home number unlisted. I wished he hadn't. He and Mom never stopped catching me by surprise, and they never would.

"Well?" he prodded.

"Are you kidding?" I asked.

"She's not out back in the garden or in her room, and she's not answering her phone. We haven't seen her since—"

"Dad, I got a job," I interrupted.

"In the music industry?" he asked.

"I'm a dog walker," I said.

There was a pause. "Hen, your mother and I are worried about you."

I laughed. "Well if it helps, I am, too."

"Are you planning on walking dogs for the rest of your life?" he asked.

"Didn't we already have a conversation like this? I feel like we did."

He exhaled deeply. "Let me just ask you a simple question. Would this job provide you with any health coverage in case, God forbid, I lost my insurance?"

Hmm. I didn't answer. I figured that if I were bitten by one of the dogs, Mrs. Abrahmson would take me to the hospital. She sounded like a nice woman.

"And how are you paid, exactly? Does your employer take taxes out?"

"It's not a career, Dad," I said. "It's a job."

"It's neither," he said. "But regardless of your grandiloquence, cash is still taxable income. You have to declare it. Otherwise, you'll have to pay a fine."

Grandiloquence? I was beginning to regret subscribing to my family's insanity. My own father was threatening me with the IRS. I hadn't even started yet.

"Things are more complicated than they seem," he added cryptically. "You're not a kid anymore."

"I'm not? Since when?"

"You're sixteen years old," he stated. "You had a bar mitzvah. You're an adult."

"According to who, your rabbi?" My voice rose. "Jesus, Dad! I can't legally drink, vote, or see an NC-17 movie in a theater. I'll be a junior in high school this fall. Say that word to yourself out loud. *Junior*. There's nothing adult about it."

"When Sarah was sixteen, she—"

"When *Sarah* was sixteen?" I spat. "*Sarah*? She's a role model now? You don't even know where she is! Maybe she ran away again!"

He sighed. "You're upset, Hen."

"I have to go, Dad. Good-bye."

I shoved my phone back into my pocket. My hands were shaking. An adult, huh? Fine. Clearly, fantasy life or no fantasy life, I *had* reached a turning point. My parents had set the terms. We were peers now. Equals. Therefore, I could act as rude, secretive, and off-the-charts psycho as they did. The solution was simple. I vowed not to speak to them again until Emma's father had secured a multimillion-dollar recording contract for Dawson's Freak. *Then* we could talk about taxable income and health coverage.

Sarah never came home that night. I pretended not to notice. I was too busy, anyway. I was employed now. I had responsibilities. *Adult* responsibilities. When I returned from Petra's, I marched straight up to my room and closed the door without saying a word to my parents.

I wasn't that upset anymore, either. I was in a strange mood. Rehearsal had left me pleasantly discombobulated.

Not surprisingly, Petra wasn't too interested in letting me compose a sensitive-but-not-cheesy ballad on a Steinway grand. Mostly she wanted to work on her own latest number, "Oedipus Wrecks." It was one of her better ones. The chorus had only one lyric, repeated sixteen straight times: "He's gonna turn his mutha out." I nailed the bass line, too, which was essentially a rip-off of Parliament Funkadelic's "Give Up the Funk." Come to think of it, the whole song was. I wasn't sure what it had to do with nineties nostalgia—it was way more seventies blaxploitation—but I had too much fun playing the riff ad nauseam to call her on it. We both did. On my way out the door, she pecked me on the cheek and said, "That was groovy. You should wear your bass lower, though, sweetie. The strap is too tight. It makes you look adult contemporary."

Funnier in writing, I reminded myself with a sigh.

I sat down at my computer.

My plan was to google old English bulldogs to see what I'd be dealing with all summer. Unfortunately I made the mistake of checking my email first.

There was a single message waiting in my in-box:

Sarah Birnbaum added you as a friend on Facebook.

I scowled at the screen, baffled. Was this a joke? I clicked on the message.

We need to confirm that you know Sarah in order for you

to be friends on Facebook.

Sarah says: "Hi, Hen. Please be my friend. I couldn't think of any other way to let you know I'm safe. Don't tell Mom and Dad that I contacted you, okay? I'll be back home as soon as I can. Don't worry about me. It will all be over soon. Love, Sarah."

To confirm this friend request, follow the link below:

http://www.facebook.com/n/?reqs/php

Thanks,

The Facebook Team

Hmm. I was used to weirdness. My entire life was weirdness. And I could have easily handled this freakish new situation in stride if it weren't for one line: "It will all be over soon." That wasn't what people said when everything was hunky-dory, or in Sarah's words, when they were "safe." It was what people said when they were about to murder a sworn enemy or detonate a bomb they were strapped to or plunge from a skyscraper. I immediately called Emma.

"Wow, that's so weird," she answered.

"You don't know the half of it," I muttered. "What's up?"

"Nothing really. I was just dialing your number again for the hundredth time. Where have you been, anyway? Your phone's off and your voice mail is full."

"I was at Petra's."

"Oh. Did you guys make out?"

I frowned. "No, Emma. We did not make out. We did

not *shtup*. Our physical intimacy was limited to one kiss. No tongue."

"You kissed on the lips?"

"Jesus, Emma! You want me to make a video next time? It was a rehearsal."

"Sorry, sorry. So what's going on?"

I stared at the screen. "I'm not really sure. My sister's gone again, but she just friended me on Facebook. She says it's the only way she can let me know she's safe. She also said, 'It will all be over soon.'"

"Whoa," Emma murmured. "What does that mean?"

"I have no idea. Do you think I should accept the friend request?"

"Are you kidding? Of course. Plus, it's bad karma not to accept a friend request on Facebook, even from stalkers."

I almost smiled. "Do you have a Facebook stalker?"

"Well, yeah," she said, as if I should obviously know.

"Who?"

"Petra, for starters," Emma said. "When you guys played at assembly in April, she sent me, like, forty messages, telling me to spread the word and make sure all my friends came. I wrote on her wall that assembly was a requirement, but it didn't stop her."

"Very funny. Anyone else?"

"That kid from your band, Bartholomew. I think he has a crush on me."

I started laughing. "What makes you think that?"

"He sent me a bunch of messages, too, asking me if I could talk to you about the dorky way you dress. Oh—and he said he liked my hair because it sticks out in a hundred different directions. He asked if I used any product."

My smile faded. "Seriously?"

"Yeah."

"You never told me that," I said.

"There's a lot I haven't told you, Hen. You have enough on your plate already."

True. And now was definitely not the time to worry about Bartholomew Savage's opinions about my wardrobe or conversations with Emma he was having behind my back. I clicked the "accept request" button and followed it to Sarah's home page. More weirdness. Her profile was completely barren—just a silhouette for a photo, no comments, no status information . . . no news on her news feed other than "*Sarah is now friends with Henry Birnbaum.*" And I was her only friend.

"Hey, why don't you come over?" Emma said. "My dad's here. You can ask him about all the exciting opportunities available in the music industry."

"Uh, no thanks," I said. "I actually found a job as a dog walker."

"Really? Cool! Woof, woof. When did that happen?"

"Just a few hours ago." Truth be told, I didn't want to run into Emma's father when I didn't have to, anyway—and not just because he was a dick. From now on, I only wanted him to see me in top form: working a crowd onstage, maybe being interviewed on *The Daily Show* or *The Colbert Report* . . . some scenario where I was impressive and in control. (Not that such a scenario had ever occurred, but it would.) "Hey, do you think if Dawson's Freak recorded a demo, your dad would listen to it?"

Emma chuckled. "I don't know. I could ask him. He's upstairs." She cupped her hand over the mouthpiece. "Hey, Dad?" she called. "Hen wants to know if you'd listen to his band's demo."

The response was muffled, but I'm pretty sure he shouted back, "Only if it makes me dance!"

"You should probably ask him when he hasn't had nine martinis," Emma said.

"Wow. That many?"

"He just got home from the airport. He's a nervous flyer."

"He did say yes, though, right?"

"Of *course*, Hen," Emma groaned. "He'd be *thrilled* to hear your demo."

I frowned again. I was about to ask her how her first day of work at the homeless shelter went, but I was suddenly too exhausted.

"*The latest twist in Hen Birnbaum's strange young life might have pushed lesser talents over the edge,*" Jim Forbes remarked. "*But Hen was too driven to let his sister's second disappearance stand in the way of success. The next morning, after a good night's sleep, he composed a song in her honor for bass and voice only, entitled*

'Please Be My Friend.' It would go on to become Dawson's Freak's third biggest hit."

"I should go to bed," I mumbled.

"Okay," Emma said gently. "Good night. Look, I know things are crazy, but don't worry about Sarah. If she says she's safe, then she's safe."

CHAPTER TEN

Bonzo and Ox

Like Petra's father, Glenda Abrahmson also lived in a renovated meat warehouse, only hers was a historic landmark. There was an actual plaque on the wall. The foundation was laid in 1898. Classy.

I arrived at 8:30 A.M. on the nose. Mrs. Abrahmson buzzed me in without bothering to ask who was there. Then I noticed a video camera above the door. The posh stairwell was carpeted, and there were paintings on the exposed brick walls: little watercolors of flowers. I wondered who owned them. The hall wasn't part of anyone's home. It was no-man's-land. But maybe if you lived in a place like this, you simply got together with your neighbors and said: "Wouldn't it be terrif if we had watercolors in our stairwell? Yes! Terrif! I'll pay. No, *I'll* pay.

No . . ." Of course, I figured I would have lots of conversations like that, once the "Please Be My Friend" royalties started pouring in. Actually, I might live in this very building. Yes. I could definitely see myself here.

An Asian woman stood at the top of the last flight of steps. She was about thirty, dressed in spandex shorts and a tight-fitting black T-shirt. Her hair was pulled back in a ponytail. She would have been gorgeous if it weren't for her bulging muscles. She was probably Mrs. Abrahmson's yoga instructor or something.

"Is that Henry?"

I paused. It was the same husky English accent I'd heard on the phone.

"Mrs. Abrahmson?" I asked.

She laughed. "That's Glenda to you."

"I . . . uh . . ."

"Who were you expecting? Some old fart?"

I shook my head. "I didn't—"

"We haven't much time," she interrupted. She opened the door. Sunlight flooded the stairwell. "I have Pilates in fifteen minutes."

I hurried after her. Puh-*what*-eez? I'd heard this word before, and knew that it had something to do with an expensive brand of exercise, but decided not to ask questions. The few rich people I knew (Emma's dad, chiefly) spoke in code, as if they had some kind of exclusive, mail-order vocabulary list. Not to worry: I'd have it soon myself.

"I ought to warn you," Mrs. Abrahmson said, stepping in front of me when I crossed the threshold. (I was too intimidated to think of her as Glenda.) She looked me straight in the eye. "I had an affair with the last dog walker. And he wasn't nearly as cute as you are. My husband had him killed."

I swallowed.

She laughed again. "Oh, I'm an awful liar. You aren't a morning person, are you? That's all right. There's a coffee shop 'round the corner on Duane Street. Wait here. I'll fetch Bonzo and Ox."

She vanished into the apartment.

I could barely see a thing. The glare was blinding. Everything was made of white marble. My eyes started to water.

"Jules!" she yelled from somewhere far away. "Hi, love. Yeah, the dog walker's here. I think I gave him a good fright."

Her voice approached. I could hear something else, too—a horrible snorting sound and the sluggish click-click-click of paws on the floor. I fought to stay composed. But when I saw what rounded the corner, I winced. These two creatures . . . they were dogs? I'd never seen anything like them: panting, slobbering, wrinkled furballs with crazed globular eyes and stumps for legs. They probably weighed more than I did. Their heads were enormous. Mrs. Abrahmson held them both on leather leashes.

"Right, right," she jabbered into her iPhone. "I—" She broke off. "Oh, dear! Your eyes are red, Henry. Are you allergic?"

I shook my head and forced a grin. "No. It's just that the sun is so bright—"

"Thank God. I thought you were a dud." She sighed. "Good thing you won't be spending any time indoors." She handed over the leashes and turned her back on me. "Look, love, he's late," she whispered. "Bring Jake up straightaway. I've got to run."

I'm not late, I felt like saying. *You said 8:30.*

I stared at the dogs. They stared back. They didn't seem particularly friendly. But who knows *what* they were? Hungry? Pissed off? I couldn't read their faces. They were unable to stop shaking and sniffling, as if they had Parkinson's disease. Their tongues hung out of their mouths.

Mrs. Abrahmson grabbed a leather purse off a marble table and shoved her iPhone inside it. "Bonzo and Oxie," she murmured in a singsong voice. She crouched beside them and scratched their heads. They didn't react. "My two little babies. Yes, yes. You're such good babies. Yes, you are."

I cleared my throat. "Um . . . so, anyway. . . ."

"Right." She straightened. "Julie will show you the ropes. She lives in the duplex downstairs. She's the other family in the advert, the one with the Lab. Well, she isn't a family. Can't be, right? She's a person." Her voice dropped to a whisper. "Her husband left her for a man, a partner at his firm. Can you imagine? Here she is."

Something moist slammed into my rear end.

I turned—and the next instant, I was being mauled by a shiny black dog the size of a football player. It tried to lick my face. I staggered backward.

"Down, Jake!" a woman cried. "Down! Down!"

She yanked the dog away.

Again I grinned. It was harder this time. I wiped Jake's drool from my nose. "Don't worry," I said. "That's okay. I love dogs."

"Jake!" Mrs. Abrahmson shrieked. "Here, boy! Here!"

"Don't encourage him," the woman said. "He's got to learn discipline." She was also wearing spandex shorts. She could have been Mrs. Abrahmson's twin, only she wasn't Asian. Her face was taut and orangey. She didn't have an ounce of fat. She handed me her leash without looking in my direction.

The two women exchanged kisses on the cheek.

The three dogs sniffed one another's butts.

I stood to the side, wishing I'd talked to Emma's dad last night about the exciting opportunities available in the music industry.

"Sorry about the rush, Jules," Mrs. Abrahmson apologized. "Just do me a favor and explain everything, all right?"

"Is the food in the usual place?" her friend asked.

"It is," Mrs. Abrahmson said. She clucked her tongue. "My, my, love. You're looking a bit worse for wear. Don't tell me you were with Otto again last night? I thought he was just a Facebook friend."

"I only have Facebook friends now. And people who follow me on Twitter. It's easier that way."

"You think?"

"Absolutely. Real friends need things."

They giggled.

Hmm. I wasn't mad, but was I missing something? Shouldn't they have acknowledged my presence by now? Shouldn't Jules or Julie or "love" have introduced herself? Etiquette might even call for an apology over how her dog had just tried to sodomize me. But, no: I was a servant. The help. I was not worthy of being addressed, except indirectly and in the third person. Silly me. Suddenly everything became very clear: These were the kind of women who went through four dog walkers a week while they rambled on and on about their fabulous lives and Puh-*what*-eez and Facebook friends with benefits with names like Otto.

These women were Petra, fifteen years from now.

I wasn't upset, though. Of course not. I was an adult. That's what Dad had called me. Anyway, there was something positive to be gained from all this. Oh, yes. I would have my revenge. They would rue the day they ignored me, once Dawson's Freak made it huge. Because I would buy this building, evict them, and turn all four floors into a massive recording studio/artistic commune/playland à la the Dandy Warhols's Odditorium. Just like Sarah wanted.

These two ditzes were going to be my biggest fans, too. Nineties nostalgia would speak their old-fart language. They were going to brag about me to all their rich friends. But I wouldn't give them any backstage passes. Nope. They would have to stand in some dank subterranean tunnel at Madison Square Garden, begging a four-hundred-pound bouncer to let them through the dressing room door, while I would look through the peephole and say, "Ha-ha-ha."

That was the plus side.

The minus side was that I probably wouldn't be playing Mrs. Abrahmson's Steinway grand anytime soon.

CHAPTER ELEVEN
Dog Run Therapy

Funny how Emma had insisted that I needed a routine this summer. Because now I had one. It was jam-packed, too. Hooray for me!

9:00 A.M. Wake up late. Panic. Take a cab into Manhattan, which eats up about $15.00, half my daily pay.

9:30 A.M. Feed the dogs in the hall outside Mrs. Abrahmson's apartment. (I am forbidden to enter, even when she is home.) Walk the dogs—a process best described as a combination of tug-of-war, screaming ("Don't eat that chicken bone!"), and public shame. Drop the dogs back at 180 Thomas Street.

10:30 A.M. Report to Gabriel's East Village crash pad for a daily bass lesson. The only "curriculum" we're able to stick to is that we do, in fact, meet daily. Argue until it becomes clear (again) that he won't give me the dirt on his and Sarah's disappearance, and then argue about the best rap rock bands of the nineties. (His top three: Limp Bizkit, Korn, and P.O.D. My top three: Beck, Kid Rock, and the Bloodhound Gang.) Privately affirm that his taste sucks.

Noon. Drag the dogs to the Warren Street dog run: a grim blacktop covered with feces and surrounded by a chain-link fence.

1 P.M. Have lunch with Emma on the lone bench at the dog run. (Conveniently, the homeless shelter is two blocks away.) Try to ignore the smell.

2 to 4 P.M. Rehearse at Sonic in preparation for the big gig. Play "Oedipus Wrecks" on average six to eight times in a row. Feel strange rush of confidence.

5 P.M. Feed the dogs dinner in the hall outside Mrs. Abrahmson's apartment, then lock them back inside.

6 to 7 P.M. Watch *Behind the Music* reruns on TiVo at Emma's. In my head, substitute the future story of Dawson's Freak with that of whatever band, phenomenon, or solo artist is being profiled.

7 P.M. Have dinner with Mom and Dad. Allow Jim Forbes to drown out any conversation.

8 to 11 P.M. Privately stress about Sarah. Hang out online in hopes of receiving a new Facebook message. Sink into depression.

11 P.M. Fall asleep without remembering to set the alarm clock.

Lunch with Emma at the dog run was by far the high point. Rehearsal wasn't bad, either, but Petra and Bartholomew Savage annoyed me. Neither of them had jobs. Nobody my age had a job besides Emma. (Nobody I knew, anyway. Even George Monroe was living it up in Europe.) Emma's job wasn't very helpful, either—at least not in terms of getting to the bottom of the Sarah mystery. The people at New Beginnings were just as shocked as we were that she'd vanished again. They hadn't seen the first disappearance coming, either. According to them, at least how Emma told it, Sarah never talked about her personal life at work other than to say, "Parents are a drag." But they were never sure if she'd been talking about her own parents or parents in general.

Not that it mattered, whichever way she meant. Those four words aren't exactly a window into a person's soul.

"You know, you're really amazing," Emma said one afternoon.

We were sitting on the bench at the dog run, munching on cheddar cheese sandwiches. (My mom always packed a lunch big enough for the both of us.) Jake, Bonzo, and Ox sniffed our laps. The cheese nearly fell out of my mouth. Emma wasn't being sarcastic. At least I was pretty sure she wasn't because of a mildly annoying trait she shared with half the planet: she brushed her hair behind her ears and said, "Umm . . ." in a dramatic voice. Not this time. I had no idea what she was talking about.

"What do you mean?" I asked.

"It's just that you stopped getting depressed," she said. She smiled, gazing over the sunbaked, poop-littered asphalt. "I mean, don't take this the wrong way, but your life sucks right now, worse than ever. You're still not sure if you're officially back in Petra's band. You still have no idea what happened to Sarah. You walk dogs for these bitchy women. But you manage to stay totally up."

"I do?"

She nodded. "Yeah. I'm kind of jealous."

Maybe I should have been an actor. "Up" was about the last thing I felt. In no particular order, my top three emotions could be listed as rage, self-pity, and bewilderment. *Everything* made me depressed. My life *did* suck. And whenever I managed to forget about it, Jim Forbes popped into my head to remind me just how much of a loser I was. *"Hen Birnbaum had hit rap rock bottom. One day he would be famous. But for now, he drowned his pain in a daily frenzy of vibrant, shameful fantasy."*

"You just have this incredible faith that everything is going to turn out for the best," she added. "I don't know how that happened, but it's nice."

"I don't know if that's true," I said.

"It must be hard. I mean, Sarah's gone again."

"Yeah. And I don't know if accepting her as a friend on Facebook was such a great idea." I wolfed down some more cheese. "I'm starting to have these weird, ultraviolent daydreams. Like Sarah and I are in some postapocalyptic battleground, and I'm hunting her down in a souped-up old truck that I turned into a tank."

"Come on, Hen," she said. "You love Sarah."

"More than life itself."

"I mean it."

I stopped chewing. "Can we not talk about Sarah?"

"She'll come home again soon," Emma said. "I know it. She's a good sister in her own way. She's generous."

"She is?" I asked.

"Do you know why New Beginnings let me be a volunteer? They don't take just anybody. But Sarah wrote me a recommendation. Well, she forged it, actually. She said she was my guidance counselor and wrote this glowing letter about how I volunteer all the time at a soup kitchen in Brooklyn and how I do all sorts of extracredit work and how I take it upon myself to help other students. For total BS, it was beautifully written."

"Really?" I frowned. "She didn't tell me that."

"It's true."

"When did she have the time?" I wondered out loud. "The whole time she was back home, she was working in our garden."

"She probably didn't want you to know," Emma said.

I believed her actually—because Sarah had done a random favor like that for me once, too. Freshman year, when I was incapacitated with food poisoning after a bad batch of Indian takeout, she offered to write a three-page paper in my name for Intro to Religion. The topic was the Almohades (pronounced ahl-mo-HAH-deez): a medieval Islamic sect famous for their vicious persecution of Jews. Sarah didn't bother doing any research. Instead she wrote about how Franklin stank at teaching religion. She argued that anybody could learn about the Almohades just by googling them; the lesson to be drawn from this assignment—and from high school education in general, which Franklin didn't seem to get—was that historical incidents weren't isolated. Writing about the Almohades wouldn't serve any purpose unless I saw their story "in a broad context, both as progenitors of the modern terrorist Islamic fringe and as part of a trend of murderous anti-Semitism dating back to Babylonia and continuing through the Holocaust." (Her words. Not too shabby, eh?) Only *then* would I actually learn something. Sarah earned me an A-plus with that crap: my first and only. My teacher said I should join the debate team. And Sarah'd never told anybody about *that*, either. At least, not that I knew of.

"I guess she is generous," I said, "but only if she can lie or prove how smart she is or get some kind of twisted pleasure out of breaking the rules while she's doing it."

Emma nodded. "You know, you're right. I've always been glad you're not like that."

I shrugged. "Me, too."

"You still love her, though," she said.

"I'm working on it."

In a way, the dog run was therapy. Emma was preparing for her newfound life's work as a social worker, and I was happy to be her guinea pig.

Sometimes we talked about our love lives (the pathetic lack

thereof). Sometimes we talked about our parents (the horror, the horror). Sometimes we took bets on how long Sarah would be AWOL this time around. (Emma was somehow convinced she'd be back in time for the gig.) But two days after the "you're really amazing" conversation, Emma asked me *why* I suddenly wanted to be a rock star. I couldn't tell if she was putting me on, but I decided to run with it. It was kind of enjoyable—like introducing myself to her all over again . . . or flirting, almost. Besides, I could make myself up as I went along.

"Because I want to bring back Satan," I said, after thinking for a minute. For some reason, Gabriel's diary had popped into my mind. "There's nothing *supernatural* about rock stars anymore. There's no evil Unseen Hand. So after Dawson's Freak is done bringing back the nineties, I'm gonna go solo and make it all about the seventies."

"Great idea. You can grow a mustache."

"And muttonchop sideburns. You know how many rumors there used to be about rock stars back in the seventies? Satan was all over the place. He was practically a member of Led Zeppelin. He was Ozzy's best friend. People used to be *scared* of Ozzy. They thought he bit the head off a bat in concert. Well, he did, but they also believed that he sacrificed a goat."

"And hung a midget," Emma said. "Don't forget that."

"Right. And then there was the one about how Gene Simmons—"

"Who?"

"The guy from KISS? They thought he worshipped Satan,

too. Anyway, the rumor was that he tossed a bucket into the audience and asked everyone to spit in it. Then he drank it. And it was common knowledge that he cut out his own tongue and had a cow's tongue sewed in its place. But look at him now. He copied Ozzy and has a wholesome family show. What happened to these guys? Where's the love for Satan?"

"I wish I knew," Emma said. "Prince of Darkness, where art thou?"

I took a deep breath. "The point is, I want to get the rumor mill churning again. 'Hey, did you hear what Hen Birnbaum did on tour in Belgium? He shot a puppy onstage and then used his evil powers to bring it back to life—and now it has rabies.' Everything's too sugarcoated now. Even Marilyn Manson's a wuss. He's a yuppie. He wrote a book."

"Are you serious?" Emma asked.

"Mm-hmm."

She shook her head. "That's so lame," she said earnestly. "Marilyn Manson should stick to movie cameos. Who's gonna write a book next? That Wiccan guy from Godsmack? Can he even spell?"

"Who knows? Satan isn't gonna help him, though."

"You got that right," Emma agreed.

"It's sad, really." I shook my head, too. When you'd hit rap rock bottom, it was nice to share life's little disappointments.

"Hen, how come you've never, ever tried to make a move on me?"

It was Friday. The noon sun was broiling hot. There was a breeze, but it didn't do much for the stale dog run smell. We were sitting on the bench eating my mom's homemade falafel. I rolled my eyes. This was a question Emma usually asked me after watching an especially gooey romantic comedy or sitcom. Thankfully, enough time had passed since my latest dream about making out with her that I could shrug it off.

"Because I like little boys," I said.

"I'm serious."

"So am I. You've seen our drummer."

"No, really," she insisted, "just tell me again. I'm bored."

"Emma," I moaned.

"Come on. Chicks need to hear these things. It's good for our self-esteem."

I sighed. "Fine. I know that if we ever fooled around, things would get really weird and tense between us. And I would never want that. Especially now." Suddenly I felt as if I were reading a cue card for a terribly written soap opera. It was pukeworthy. I could do a lot better. "On second thought, maybe we should just go ahead and hook up. We're both still virgins. It's not healthy. My dad says I'm an adult." I shoved the rest of the falafel in my mouth and grinned. "What do you think?"

"No way," she said. She looked very pleased with herself. "It would be too weird and tense."

"Why?" I asked, suddenly interested in the conversation and half wishing Gabriel were here to overhear it. "What *would* be weird and tense about it, anyway? I mean, everybody says: Fooling around with certain friends is weird. But I think that's just an old wives' tale—you know, like how playing with yourself will make you go blind."

"Have you ever hooked up with a friend before, Hen?"

"Wait. Who said that? I can't see you!"

She laughed. "Seriously."

"Does Petra count? Aside from her, I don't really have that many female friends."

"Well, trust me. Hooking up with a friend is always bad news." She paused for a long moment. There was a strange lilt in her voice I'd never heard before. "There's no such thing as friends with benefits. *That's* an old wives' tale."

I stared at her. She turned to Bonzo and Ox. She seemed to be waiting for something. Her chest rose and fell in an even rhythm under her T-shirt. All at once, the smelly, stagnant air of the dog run felt charged; atoms were whirling faster, humming with energy. But, no, I was imagining things. She wasn't suggesting that she *wanted* me to make a move. Of course she wasn't. Not now, after an eternity, out of the blue. Not with falafel on my breath, and the sun beating down, and midday traffic honking on the street. We were in public, for God's sake. Besides, she had to go back to work. She was teasing me, rattling me, trying to throw a wrench in our monotonous little summer routine. So she created a little phony lunchtime innuendo. Like she said, she was bored.

She stood up. "I shouldn't eat your mom's falafel in the

middle of the day. It's awesome, but it makes me all logy. I'll see you later, Hen."

"Wait. When have you ever hooked up with a friend?"

She smiled at me. "Are you kidding?"

"So you were messing with my head."

"Of course I was. That's what we do. We mess with each other's heads. What are you, on drugs right now?"

"Yes, Emma," I said. "Yes, I am. I use them as a cry for help."

"Well I'm here for you, my friend. Take one day at a time. Remember: When you try to escape from reality, you're only escaping from yourself."

She winked at me and strolled out of the dog run. I watched her disappear around the corner, her ratty hair flapping in the breeze. The atoms began to slow down. But then, they'd never sped up in the first place. At least, I was pretty sure they hadn't.

CHAPTER TWELVE

Beer Tasting

About a week and a half after Sarah disappeared for the second time, she began updating her Facebook news feed in a sudden frenzy.

Sarah Birnbaum thinks it's a travesty that certain airlines charge for snacks on international flights.

Sarah Birnbaum wishes that sunscreen didn't come in stinky lotion form.

Sarah Birnbaum hopes to make it back in time to see **Henry** play his big gig.

Sarah Birnbaum believes everyone in life deserves a second chance, even former Nazis. Especially if they buy you orchids.

I received all four updates on the same afternoon in the space of an hour. She was sort of brilliant, my sister. I understood the plan now. This was our private line. Since she wasn't Facebook friends with anyone else, I was the only person who could read her posts. And as far as she was concerned, they told me everything I needed to know: That she *was* safe, that she'd returned to the Dominican Republic for some reason, and that she wouldn't be gone for a year this time. They also told me that she was in communication with Gabriel. Who else could have told her about the gig?

And thanks to Gabriel's manuscript, I also knew a few other things she *didn't* know I knew. Like the name of the flower-buying Nazi, for one: Karl Funkhausen. (Unless she knew more than one Nazi? Yikes.) But in a way, the stuff I wasn't supposed to know only made me more frustrated. Even with the new puzzle pieces, I couldn't form a clear picture. Sarah was too cautious and clever. So was Gabriel.

Of course, he had the added drawback of being someone I saw in person. Plus, I generally wanted to punch him in the face after spending any time with him.

Jesus. What about me? This wasn't exactly bringing out the best parts of my personality. The longer it went on, the more I felt like Encyclopedia Freaking Brown. Only dorkier. And not as upstanding. After all, I was a thief, too.

The morning after I received Sarah's flurry of updates, Gabriel threw a zinger at me. "Hen, your playing is getting better. You know that?"

I was packing up to leave his East Village crash pad after one of our more productive lessons. He and I had managed to play along to all of "Motown Philly" by Boyz II Men without messing up once. Triumph! But still, I hadn't expected a compliment.

"You think?" I asked him.

Gabriel nodded. "You're not just playing the notes. You're listening now. You're feeling the music."

"Please don't say stuff like that," I grumbled. "It was Boyz II Men."

He laughed. "I know. I wanted to see if you could groove on a song you hated. I really wish I could come see your gig, man." He glanced down at his plain white T-shirt and frayed jeans. "It would also give me an excuse to buy some new clothes."

Aha! I thought. Could this be a way in? "You're still having legal troubles?" I asked nonchalantly.

"Something like that," he said.

I zipped up my bass case and leaned against the door. "Hey, can I ask you something? What made you decide to go with the whole nineties nostalgia thing, anyway? I mean, for your band?"

"It wasn't my idea." He sat on the edge of the futon. "It was Rich, my guitarist's. Actually, Madeline came up with the name. They used to be a couple."

"Really? Was that weird for you?"

"What do you mean?" he asked.

"Uh . . . just that, you know, you said you used to be in love

146

with Madeline," I stammered. "Or something like that."

He sighed. "I guess it was weird. The whole thing was weird. Rich and Madeline and Tony, our drummer, were obsessed with *Friends*. They used to skip classes to watch it. The three of them. Tony was their third wheel. They didn't seem to mind, though." His eyes darted over to his laptop, perched on top of the pile of manuscripts. "Tony's a big computer geek. He was able to steal all sorts of things off the internet. He got them every single episode of *Friends* on DVD delivered for free."

Now we're getting somewhere, I thought.

"Why are you smiling?" Gabriel asked.

"Uh . . . just, um, that's funny," I said. "Our drummer is a computer geek, too."

"Yeah." Gabriel nodded thoughtfully. "It makes sense. Drums and computers are technical. Drums are, like, the math requirement of music."

"You're not a math person, huh?"

He shook his head. "It's sort of pathetic. Columbia has a math requirement, and I nearly flunked out because of it. Sarah, too. We both got straight As in religion and philosophy and our writing seminars . . ." His voice trailed off. "You know, it was Sarah who came up with our band motto. 'Friend is not a verb.' It was hilarious."

"It was?" I heard myself ask. Whoops. I should have kept my mouth shut. I wanted him to relax and forget himself.

Gabriel flashed a lopsided grin. "You sort of had to be there, I guess. She went off on this whole speech about how the era of good, smart lyrics was over. She said that people didn't know how to be intimate anymore, because of the internet. All the new popular bands—you know, like the Jonas Brothers and the Cheetah Girls—all their hit songs were about IMs and email and texting. There was nothing face-to-face about them. Nothing *real*. Friendship had lost its substance. Once she articulated it like that, it sort of cemented our nineties nostalgia thing."

"Wow," I said. "Profound." I cringed. I actually meant it, but the word came out sounding smug and sarcastic.

"Ah . . . I'm boring you," Gabriel said. "You should probably get going."

"No, no—you're not boring me at all," I protested.

"Maybe." Gabriel grinned at me again. "But you know, Hen, you're still not going to trick me into telling you why Sarah and I ran away."

Six days before the gig, Emma showed up unannounced at band practice, carrying a grocery sack. Apparently, New Beginnings didn't need her to volunteer in the afternoons anymore. Mornings only. Bartholomew Savage and Petra were understandably irritated—so was I—until she pulled out a six-pack of beer.

"Musicians need booze," she declared.

Bartholomew Savage's face lit up. Both Petra and I passed on the offer. (I needed to become a rock star *before* I became a raging alcoholic.) Emma cracked open a can for him and one for herself, then sat cross-legged in the corner of the stuffy little room. "Don't mind me," she said. "Keep jamming."

"Did you get a fake ID?" I asked.

"It's my cousin Nadine's. I showed you, remember?"

I didn't, but I didn't feel like solving another mystery right now. Emma sat quietly for the remainder of the rehearsal, drinking beer after beer. Bartholomew stopped at two. Emma finished the rest. When our time was up, she lumbered to her feet and clapped loudly.

"Awesome!" she slurred. "Is it my imagination, or is it 1993 in here? Give it up, people!"

Bartholomew Savage laughed. Petra forced a smile. I blinked at her, lost.

"You really think we sound good?" Petra asked.

"I'd tell you if I didn't. My inhibitions are at a Nadine." She hiccupped. "I mean a nadir."

The following day, Emma showed up again at Sonic Rehearsal Studios with another six-pack. Nobody protested. Nobody even said hi. Emma simply cracked open a beer for Bartholomew Savage, and one for herself, and sat cross-legged in the corner.

Interesting. For whatever reason, she was part of the routine now. We had a drunken groupie. Good for us. I only hoped she didn't develop cirrhosis of the liver.

Monday night, with two days to go, Petra invited everybody over to my place to strategize about gig promotion. (Both her mom and her dad were throwing separate parties that night, so their apartments were off-limits.) We all crammed into my room. Petra and Bartholomew Savage sat on the edge of my bed; I sat at my desk . . . and, yes, Emma joined the party, too. She sat on the floor in the corner. Luckily, she only brought one beer this time. She'd hidden it in a brown paper bag, so my parents wouldn't see. Not that the bag did anything to mask the smell.

"So what do you think of the Facebook fan page I set up for Dawson's Freak?" Petra asked, all business.

I turned on my computer and linked to it, taking the hint. It *was* pretty funny. She'd found an old *Dawson's Creek* cast photo and photoshopped our faces onto it. She was Katie Holmes's character. Bartholomew Savage was the handsome blond star, Dawson. And I was the pudgy one. (What was his name? Pacey?)

"I re-friended all my friends from the band page and updated the news feed last night," she added, as if we needed reminding. "I'll do it again tonight and tomorrow. So hopefully we'll get a good crowd."

"Easy there, Petra," Emma said. "You're stalking me again." She turned to me. "See? What did I tell you?"

Petra didn't seem to get the joke. I didn't blame her. But my mind was elsewhere. For the first time, I felt a little flutter of nervous anticipation. The gig was really happening.

"Everything changed the night of the Bimbo Lounge show," Jim Forbes remarked. *"The club was packed with celebrities and representatives from every record company on the East Coast. Eddie Vedder offered to be their manager. A bidding war began on the*

spot. Fortunately, their lawyer, Mr. Donovan Wood, Esquire, was able to sign the band to a multimillion-dollar deal the very next day . . ."

"Hey, do you think there's a chance your dad would come to the show tomorrow night?" I asked Emma.

"About as much chance as you have of hooking up with one of those Fox News Sexperts," she said.

"Ha-ha. He goes to shows all the time for business. You told me he goes out at least one night a week."

"Right." She took a sip of beer. "For business. Not to see Dawson's Geek."

"Dawson's *Freak*," Petra corrected.

"I *know*, Petra," Emma groaned.

"He said he wanted to hear a demo," I pointed out. "If he wants to hear a demo, wouldn't he want to see us live?"

"I told you, he was drunk when he said that."

"He only had nine martinis, right? How drunk are *you* right now?"

"Ha! Let me explain something to you, Hen. My dad's clients play at Giants Stadium. Not the Bimbo Lounge."

"Nada Surf plays at Giants Stadium?" I asked. "Where? In the men's room?"

"Okay, look," Emma said. "You want to know the truth? Even if my dad *did* come and see you play, he wouldn't remember it."

"What do you mean? Why not?"

"He drinks too much, Hen! There's no way he'd come to

see you play unless he was loaded. Not to mention the fact that he hates rap rock. He wouldn't get the irony. He's going to see Journey because he genuinely enjoys their music."

"Well, maybe he'd enjoy ours," I said angrily.

She shrugged. "Whatever."

Petra didn't look so happy anymore. "What do you think we should put on the flyers?" she asked me.

"And that's another thing," Emma said. "If I were you guys, I wouldn't waste money making flyers."

"Waste money?" Petra repeated.

Emma nodded. "That's right. Flyers don't work."

"I found a job because of a flyer," I pointed out.

"And look how wonderful it is. Look, the best way to promote a gig is to tell all your friends. But no offense, Hen, you don't have any friends besides the people in this room. You're *looking* at your audience. And two of them are already in the band."

"How many friends do *you* have, Emma?" I snapped.

She rolled her eyes. "I don't want to be a famous rock star, Hen. Come on, do you really think that people are gonna want to shell out eight bucks or whatever it is to see your band play at some dump? On a Wednesday?"

I frowned. Lots of people had seen PETRA the one time we'd performed at school. Then again, attendance at the assembly we'd played had been mandatory. There hadn't been a cover charge, either.

"I'm sorry," Emma said. "Look, I don't want to be a Negative

Nelly, I swear. And I would have tried to get people at work to come, but I don't think homeless people make enough money to go out on weeknights. I know volunteers don't."

Petra scowled. "Emma, why are you so catty around me? Can't you say one nice thing for once? Like, 'Hey, guys, way to go. I think it's great you got a gig.'"

Emma laughed and looked at me again. "Because if I said that, I wouldn't be fulfilling my god-given role as the only realist in this strange little posse."

I knew she was expecting me to laugh, too. But I didn't give her the satisfaction. I didn't even smile, and I was proud of myself. It meant that I *had* grown up a little this summer. Emma might have morphed into a surly, intolerable booze-hound, but she could no longer cajole me into having fun at my own expense.

"You know, I was thinking about something," Bartholomew Savage said. "We should just make our demo off the sound board at the show. Victor said they have a really good system there. My dad got me ACID Pro, and I . . ."

"Donovan Wood never made it to that first gig," Jim Forbes said.

Thankfully, the comment drowned out Bartholomew Savage's rambling monologue. Once he started talking about computers, he wouldn't shut up. Blah, blah, blah. He never understood that the average layman has no interest in sequencing and layering . . . it was all technical mumbo jumbo. On the other hand, I had complete faith in his abilities. If he claimed he could produce a first-rate demo, then he would. He'd opted to take elective computer courses at Spencer, the way normal people at Franklin opted to take fun elective courses like Knitting, or the Literature and Films of Woody Allen.

"When their lawyer listened to the recording from the show, there was no turning back," Jim Forbes went on. *"Donovan Wood knew a sure bet when he heard one. Dawson's Freak had captured a sound like no other, at the right time, in the right place—"*

"Beer tasting *is* a good idea!" Bartholomew Savage exclaimed.

I glanced around the room.

"It makes sense, right?" Emma said. "I mean, just as many people drink beer as they do wine. Beer deserves the same snootiness."

Everyone was smiling. Apparently, Bartholomew Savage wasn't talking about computers anymore. I didn't know *what* he was talking about. This kind of thing had happened a few times before in the last few days. I'd zone out with Jim Forbes for a minute or two—and before I knew it, the tension would be gone and Emma and Petra and Bartholomew Savage would be sharing a new inside joke that I'd completely missed. I tried to smile along, but I felt as if I had tuned into a zany new reality show whose premise I didn't understand. The fresh, fuzzy glow of the evening was beyond my reach. And I couldn't ask them to repeat what they had said or I'd look like a moron. I wondered if this was what Gabriel had felt around Rich and Madeline and Tony.

"You'd have to use the same language as a wine tasting," Petra said. "You'd have to describe the beer the way you'd describe a person. You know?"

"It's an *aggressive* beer," Emma suggested, "but coquettish at the same time."

"Yes," Bartholomew Savage agreed. "It skips the foreplay and goes straight for the intercourse."

"Right, right," Emma said. She sat up straight, eyeing her bagged bottle thoughtfully. "Drinking this beer is like making love to a butch lesbian in prison."

The three of them laughed together. "Haw, haw, haw. Hee, hee, hee."

I tried to smile. It didn't really work. Nice. I was a loser and outsider in my own home. No big deal, though. I was still excited about the gig. Like Emma had said, I was "up." Or I could pretend to be. Dawson's Freak had begun its rocket ride to the top. We would blow everyone's minds Wednesday night—and then Emma and Petra would forget all about beer tasting or prison sex or whatever it was their new girl club plus one was talking about. They'd only remember I was the glue that bound our strange little posse together.

The morning of the gig, Gabriel offered me these ridiculous words of advice: "When you're onstage tonight, don't look out at the audience until halfway through your second song. Then make eye contact with Emma."

I was sitting on the edge of his futon, plucking out the

"Oedipus Wrecks" riff for the nine hundredth time. He was nodding his head in rhythm, sipping a Bloody Mary.

"And why on earth would I do that?" I asked.

"Because that's how long it generally takes for the wall of make-believe to go up. Once it's up, you can see the truth."

I glanced up at him. "Did you start drinking before I got here?"

He laughed and scratched his belly through his flimsy T-shirt. "Every gig you play has a wall of make-believe," he stated. "It goes up when you're pretty well into it. It's that magical point when the people you're performing for, your closest friends, actually *buy* into the role you're all playing. You're the professional musician, putting on a show. They're the audience members, digging it. At that moment, you *are* a rock star."

My fingers began to ache. I stopped playing. "Do you think maybe you could talk to me the way normal people talk for once?" I asked tiredly. "You know, instead of like some cult leader or infomercial scam artist?"

He upended the glass and drained it, then plunked it on top of the amp, where it teetered dangerously for a few seconds before wobbling to a standstill. "You sound a lot like Sarah sometimes," he said with a sigh.

Ugh. Reminding him of my sister was definitely not territory I wanted to explore. "Hey, speaking of Sarah, do you have any idea when she'll be back?" I asked flatly.

He flashed me his usual, half-apologetic, half–Cheshire

Cat grin. There were bits of tomato juice stuck in his teeth. "Soon, I hope. This wasn't part of the plan. We were supposed to figure this part out together."

"Oh, yeah? Go on. I'm listening."

"Aren't you more interested in learning how the wall of make-believe allows you to see the truth?" he asked. "It'll be important for tonight."

I blinked at him several times, my jaw clenched.

"I guess not," he said. "Well, I'll tell you, anyway. That's the kind of bass teacher I am. See, there will be a moment tonight where Emma will feel safe enough to show you how she really feels. You onstage, her in the audience . . . Just watch her body language. That's when you'll *know*. If you wait until the middle of the second song, then look up, smile, and make eye contact—"

"I'm a lot more interested in talking about Sarah," I interrupted.

"We are, in a way. Just let me finish." He grabbed his glass and plodded into the kitchen and opened the refrigerator. As always, my eyes guiltily darted toward the pile of manuscripts. It was a reflex I should really learn to quash. I'd make a terrible criminal. I *was* a terrible criminal. "The moment I'm describing . . . I had it with Sarah at the last gig Friends ever played," he said. I could hear him refilling his drink, the quiet chug-chug-chug of a big bottle of vodka. "We never talked about it. But I still *know*."

"Know *what*?" I demanded.

"That we were more than just friends, and we always would be."

I tossed the bass onto the mattress. "So let me get this straight. If I look at Emma in the middle of the second song at the gig tonight, and make eye contact with her, I'll know she really *is* the cheese to my macaroni."

"Yes! You're catching on."

My shoulders sagged. I was too fed up to be annoyed anymore. "Fine. But let's make a bet, all right? If I do everything you say, and there's no magic moment between Emma and me, then tomorrow, you *have* to tell me why you and Sarah ran away and came back. Okay?"

He poked his head around the corner. His rheumy eyes twinkled. "I'm sorry, Hen. I'm not the gambling sort. I deal in absolutes."

"Jesus, Gabriel."

"All right, I'll tell you this. If you want to understand why Sarah and I came back, read *No Exit* by Jean-Paul Sartre. Then you'll know."

No Exit, I thought to myself, suppressing a puzzled grin. Coincidentally enough, I *had* read it—for Intro to Philosophy last year. "Isn't that about a bunch of dead people trapped in hell?" I asked him.

He smiled sadly. "Exactly, Hen. That's exactly what it is. And I think that ends our bass lesson for today."

CHAPTER THIRTEEN
Underage Talent Night

Emma was right: The Bimbo Lounge *was* a dump.

When I first walked through the door, I honestly thought that I had made some kind of mistake—that the club had moved from its original location, or that they were renovating . . . or *something*. This couldn't be the place, the famous underground spot where David Bowie had played an impromptu acoustic set. It was smaller than my living room. The floor was strewn with cigarette butts—odd, as smoking in bars is illegal in New York. The bar against the right-hand wall was only about ten feet long.

"Hello?" I called.

Nobody answered. I shivered—partly from nervousness, and partly because it was so cold. The air-conditioning was cranked. It felt like a walk-in freezer. I shifted my bass case from one hand to the other and peered toward the tiny stage in back. Bartholomew Savage had promised me that I wouldn't need to bring my awesome bass rig. He and Petra were still outside, unloading our equipment from a cab. But all I could see were two monitors, two mic stands, and a tangled web of wires. There were no amplifiers. Where would I plug in? Would I have to rush back home to get my rig? Even if I did, I couldn't see where I would put it. The stage didn't look big enough for a drum kit, let alone anything else . . .

"Oi!" a voice barked.

I jumped. A punk rocker poked his head out of the small sound booth next to the door. He looked and sounded exactly like Sid Vicious from the Sex Pistols. The resemblance was shocking. He had the same ghoulish complexion and spiky hair; he even had the same chain-and-padlock necklace.

"Nobody's allowed in till eight," he growled.

"But I'm playing tonight," I answered meekly. I waved my bass case, as if to prove it.

"You Spacetime Logic?"

I blinked.

"What *band*?" he snapped.

"Dawson's Freak," I said.

He laughed. "Right. Victor's little brother's band." Something in his tone suggested that the Bimbo Lounge might as well have booked a sock puppet show to fill the eight o'clock slot. He disappeared down a hidden stairwell. It was strange;

my life was inexplicably top-heavy with British assholes: this guy, Mrs. Abrahmson . . .

The door opened. Bartholomew shambled past me with his kick drum case and dumped it onstage. I felt better with him around. He was practically family at this place. His presence lent mine credibility. And in the red light, he really looked amazing. He'd spiked his hair. He was wearing leather pants. Bartholomew Savage was the only kid I knew who could wear leather pants and still be taken seriously by girls. I probably should have tried to dress up a little more. I was wearing a pair of old brown cords and a black T-shirt: the same outfit I had been wearing all day. I looked like a geek and smelled like an old English bulldog.

"Did you meet Sid?" Bartholomew Savage asked.

My eyes narrowed. "The sound guy?"

He nodded, then tiptoed over and leaned close to me. "His accent is fake," he whispered. "He's really from Great Neck. His name is Isaac Mendel. But he's got mad skills. He worked on an Elefant record."

Wonderful. Yet another lunatic in our midst. A lunatic responsible for engineering our demo, no less. But at least he had "mad skills." I put down my bass and followed Bartholomew Savage back onto the street. The evening sun seemed much hotter. Petra scrambled to gather her guitar and amplifier and effects pedals, but she could hardly manage. I stacked the last of the drum cases. All of us began to sweat.

"Hey . . . uh, can I ask you guys something?" I said. "Is

there a bass rig in there somewhere?"

Bartholomew Savage shook his head. "The bass always goes direct at Bimbo."

Now I was scared. I'd never gone direct before: straight through a sound board, without any intermediary amplification. It didn't seem right, somehow. A big electric bass needed a big bass amp.

"You sure that'll work?" I asked, trailing him back inside.

"Yeah, yeah," he mumbled. I couldn't tell if he was trying to shut me up, or if he really knew what he was talking about. Despite the fact that Bartholomew Savage was two years younger than me, I always felt like a little boy around him. At fourteen, he'd already nailed the mature swagger of someone always on top of his game—a swagger I was certain would elude me until we were all rock stars (which we would be, soon enough).

Sid started setting up the mic stands. Petra and Bartholomew Savage joined him onstage. They had their own equipment to prepare. But I didn't. All I had was my bass. I dropped off the drum cases and stood in the middle of the room, eyeing Petra. She'd dressed up for the gig, too. The ensemble was sort of painful: an oversized flannel shirt over a black cocktail dress, complete with a black wool cap, just like Emma had foretold. Was it a costume? Was it ironic? I couldn't even tell anymore.

"'Ow many mics ya need, Bart?" Sid asked.

"Just one," I said.

"I was talking to Bart," Sid said.

Nobody spoke after that. As far as I could tell, the other

three were pretending to be extra busy so that I would feel use-less—connecting cables, tightening screws, mounting drum microphones. I cast a longing gaze toward the exit.

"You wankers expecting a good crowd?" Sid asked. He carried one of the mic stands offstage.

Bartholomew Savage looked at me. Evidently, Sid wasn't directing questions at him anymore. "Pretty good," I piped up. I was lying.

"We set up a Facebook page," Petra said. "We have two hundred eighty friends."

Sid seemed unimpressed. "You gotta draw at least fifty real people if you wanna get booked here again. Did you make flyers?"

Petra and I exchanged a quick glance. I knew what she was thinking: *If only Emma hadn't opened her mouth . . .* After her little Monday night rant, we'd felt too self-conscious to do anything other than update the news feed and pray for people to show.

"Army of the Night didn't make flyers either," Sid said. "Ever hear of them?"

Petra and I shook our heads.

"Of course you didn't, wankers. 'Cause they didn't make flyers. But, hey, it ain't my fault if you don't get another gig." Sid headed toward the sound booth. "There's a direct box on the floor," he muttered to me. "Plug in there."

"Hey, what's the drinking policy?" I asked quickly. "Do bands drink for free?"

He sneered. "One soda, one Bud, or one Bud Light on tap. You pay for the rest. But that's a moot point, mate. You're underage and the bartender ain't here. Now get onstage. You want a sound check or not?"

I swallowed. No beverages, no bass rig . . . the night was already falling apart, and it hadn't even started. It was a very good thing that Emma's dad didn't know about this show. We could treat it as another rehearsal, preparing for the real deal: the big gig when we changed Donovan Wood's life. The Bimbo Lounge was too small for us, anyway.

I took out my bass and slung it over my shoulder, then jumped onstage and plugged it into the tiny little black box on the floor. The instrument's neck swung like a wrecking-ball crane, slamming into the hi-hat stand. Bartholomew Savage glared at me. "Oops," I murmured. I grinned sheepishly and stood up straight. I had about six inches in either direction. If I moved too far to the left, I would bump into one of the crash cymbals. Too far to the right, I would fall off the stage.

"Play something," Sid ordered. His voice blared from the monitors.

I peered into the dim red haze. Sid was only about twenty feet from me, but he looked very small and far away, hunched behind the sound board. I turned up the volume and plucked the E string. Nothing happened. I plucked it again. Still nothing.

"'Ow's that sound?" he asked.

I shook my head. "I can't hear it," I yelled.

He frowned and adjusted some knobs. There was a screech of feedback. I winced.

"Try again," he commanded. "And speak into the mic."

I plucked the E string one more time. I could hear a faint rumble now, but it was distant and toneless, as if it were coming from another building.

"I'm sorry," I said into the microphone. "Could I just get a little more bass in the monitor?"

"Oi!" His voice boomed back at me. "You think I don't know how it sounds up there? I engineered Shaquille O'Neal's last album. Now let's hear the kick drum."

I glanced at Bartholomew Savage. He was still glaring at me. I figured that meant my part of the sound check was over.

The bartender didn't arrive until 7:50. She was about thirty-five, with a hard face and heavy black eyeliner. Steal Your Parents' Money was tattooed down her arm in tiny gothic letters.

I smiled at her. I told her that I was the bassist for Dawson's Freak and that I wanted to cash in my one Coke on tap. She didn't say a word. Her face registered no response. Maybe she was a deaf-mute. She drew the Coke, though. I guzzled it while Petra and Bartholomew Savage argued with Sid about the process of recording our show.

"All we need is a quarter-inch adapter," Petra said.

"That still doesn't solve the problem," Sid said.

"It does if you bypass the effects loop," Bartholomew Savage said.

I tuned them out and finished my free soda. Then I bought one. For once, Jim Forbes had nothing to say. I calculated how much this gig was costing me: seventeen bucks for the cab ride each way, a two-dollar soda so far . . . far more than I made in a day walking Bonzo and Ox. I was *losing* money. Petra and Sid and Bartholomew Savage kept talking. The room was deserted. I wondered where Emma was. She wouldn't have flaked on this . . . would she?

By 8:15, the only other people who showed were the members of Spacetime Logic, the band who was due to take the stage after us. They were all wearing black suits with skinny ties: an eighties nostalgia act, from what I could tell. They looked like jackasses. I began to get panicky. Finally, when I'd resigned myself to the fact Emma had decided not to come and that I hated her and we'd never be friends again ever, she strolled leisurely through the door. It was almost 8:30. Her hair was rattier than usual. She looked as if she'd tumbled out of bed. Literally. She was wearing a pajama top over a T-shirt.

"Hello, Cleveland!" she said, sitting on the stool beside me. "Hey, how come I'm not on the guest list?"

"I don't think there is a list," I said.

"There's always a list." She looked around and smirked. "What's with the red lights? Do they develop photos in here, too? Like as an incentive to keep customers on the premises?"

"Emma, I'm really not in the mood," I muttered.

"Sorry, sorry," she said. "So what's with the long face? Are you nervous?"

"Nah. I'm just conducting my own little soda-tasting here."
I took a sip and arched an eyebrow. "This one tastes like a guy
who spent all night in the gutter."

She stopped smiling. "Hen, seriously. You didn't get wasted
for the first time in your life or anything did you? I've quit
drinking, myself."

A hand clamped down on my shoulder.

"Time to start, mate," Sid growled in my ear. "I ain't waitin'
around all night."

Petra and Bartholomew Savage were already climbing
onstage. I glanced around the bar. There were a total of nine
people present, including Sid and the bartender. Nine. Forty-
one less than the number we needed to get booked here again.
Forty-three if you didn't count employees; forty-seven if you
didn't count the other band. An audience of three, basically:
Emma, plus a twentysomething couple I'd never seen before.

And no Sarah, obviously. Of course not. She'd "hoped" to
get home in time for the gig, but she just hadn't "hoped" hard
enough. Too bad. Because I'd been harboring a particularly
idiotic fantasy, too shameful even to share really, but what
the hell . . . I'd fantasized that Gabriel *was* right, that a wall
of make-believe *would* go up (though not in the way he'd
predicted) and that Sarah and I would make eye contact, and
she would suddenly realize—while basking in the mellifluous
thud of my Godlike bass riffs (like I said: idiotic fantasy)—
that it was beyond cruel to hide anything anymore to her little
brother . . . and as soon as the show was over, she would drag

me off the stage and confess, confess, confess.

Well. So much for all that. And Emma was wrong. Getting wasted for the first time in my life probably would have been a great idea. I slunk off the barstool and took my place next to the crash cymbal.

The lights went up.

At first I couldn't see a thing. I squinted into a shadowy reddish-black void. After a few seconds, my eyes began to adjust to the glare. I wish they hadn't.

"Woo-hoo!" Emma cried, clapping. She was the only one making any noise. "Rock and roll, baby! Who loves the nineties? We do! *Viva las noventa!*"

I caught a glimpse of her, standing by the bar. She was in a great mood, wasn't she? Of course: She'd predicted that we would bomb. Then her smile widened. Uh-oh. Bad sign. I knew that look in her eye; I knew exactly what she was about to do. Ten-to-one she would also do it at the Journey concert two nights from now to rag on her father. But tonight was different. Tonight she *was* her father. The transformation was complete; all she lacked was the gelatinous neck.

Don't do it, I silently begged. *Please—*

"Disco sucks!" she howled gleefully. She thrust her right fist in the air, pinky and forefinger raised in the heavy-metal horn salute. "Disco sucks!"

The set was a disaster. If a wall of make-believe had gone up, it didn't do anyone present any good. I couldn't hear a thing except the drums and Petra's piercing vocals. But I went through the motions as gamely as I could, struggling to keep my balance so I wouldn't fall off the stage—until my D string broke. It was one of the few times the bass was audible. We were nearing the end of our only cover (a stripped-down version of Beck's "Loser") when there was a pop, and Petra's guitar went horrendously out of tune. She grimaced at me, eyes blazing. It took me a second to realize that it wasn't her guitar; it was my bass, but the mix was so bad that I couldn't tell one instrument from the other.

I sat out for the remainder of the song. Somewhere in there I snuck a frightened peek at the nearly deserted room, and I noticed Emma was missing. (So much for Gabriel's big momentous prediction for us. He truly *was* a jackass, wasn't he?) Then I tried playing the last two numbers with three strings. I kept hitting bad notes. It didn't matter, though; the sound was mush, and there was a huge commotion at the door, and nobody was listening anyway. As I later found out, some of Bartholomew Savage's friends were trying to get in, but for reasons unknown the bouncer had suddenly decided to start carding at 9:30.

Underage Talent Night was officially over.

When I walked off the stage, Emma was still nowhere to be seen. I spent several minutes staring at the women's room door, waiting for her to walk out. The bartender walked out instead.

So. Emma had split before the show was over. No goodbye. Not even a wave. She'd vanished. Just like Sarah. Ha! Was there a pattern forming? Maybe it was something about *me* . . .

Petra rushed over, looking harried. "Hey, Hen?" she said, handing me her guitar case. "Can you do me a huge favor and drop this off at my dad's apartment? Just let yourself in again. The door's open. I want to go back to Bartholomew's place to see if there's anything salvageable for a demo."

I nodded absently. The sinking emptiness in my stomach began to spread in waves through my body.

"Hey, are you okay?" she asked.

I nodded, heaving her guitar onto my other shoulder. With both my bass and Petra's guitar, I looked like a hunchback. I felt like one, anyway.

"Don't worry," Petra murmured. "The show wasn't that bad. I'll call you later, okay, sweetie? Bye." She pecked me on the cheek and raced out the door.

Not that bad? I wondered.

I hobbled over to the bar, where the bartender was wiping out empty mugs with a dishtowel.

"Can I please have a Coke?" I said.

"No," she replied. It was the first time she had spoken all night. She didn't even look up. She kept right on wiping.

"Um, excuse me?" I shook my head, flabbergasted.

"Get it somewhere else," she said. "You should have seen yourself onstage, all off balance and whatnot. I can't believe you didn't fall off. It pisses me off that kids think they can smuggle in their own booze."

I had to laugh. "I hate to break it to you, ma'am, but I didn't smuggle in anything. Not even my own water. And it's sort of hard to keep your balance when there's no room on your teeny little stage, ma'am, because—"

"Ma'am? What am I, your grandma? Look, no offense, but I'm just saying that your body doesn't look as if it can handle any more alcohol."

My body doesn't look . . . Okay. No problem. No offense taken. I turned and stomped toward the door, with the sole intention of buying a lighter and several gallons of kerosene and returning to burn the Bimbo Lounge to the ground—but one of the guys from Spacetime Logic stopped me.

"Hey, bro, that was a cool set," he said.

"Ha-ha," I muttered. I tried to brush past him. He stood in my way.

"What, dude?" he said. "I loved it. Especially that song about Oedipus."

"Really?" The tension in my jaw started to ease slightly. "You mean it?"

"Yeah. You know, it's weird. You guys sound a lot like we did when Atlantic was interested in us. We sucked back then." He grinned. "So, hey—what's your singer's name?"

"Petra Dostoyevsky," I said.

"Petra what?"

"Dostoyevsky. Like the Russian novelist."

"Oh. Cool. Is she seeing anybody?"

I frowned. "Not that I know of."

"Well, look, bro, can you do me a favor? Friend me on

Facebook. My Facebook name is Brian Hussein Singer. Then recommend her as a friend."

"What? Why?"

"Why?" He laughed loudly, and then stared at me as if I were an idiot. "Because I wanna bang her, dude. She's totally hot."

CHAPTER FOURTEEN
The Aftermath

When I finally made it to Petra's dad's loft that night—after telling Sid to screw off when he asked me to pay him for the recording (the first time in my life I'd ever told off a stranger, and it felt pretty freaking awesome, thank you), after nearly giving myself a hernia schlepping both guitars up the long, rickety stairwell . . . after all *that*, I pushed through the unlocked steel door to find a strange black man in the middle of the room.

I rubbed my eyes, hoping he would disappear. He didn't. He was real, all right, standing beside one of the longer couches, reading a piece of folded paper. *What the hell?* He was maybe ten years younger than my parents, bearded and unkempt, dressed in some kind of hippie poncho and one of those ridiculous green wool Rastafarian caps.

He glanced at me. "What's up, chief?" he said.

I figured I had three options. One: I could smash him over the head with either Petra's guitar or my bass. But that might be messy, and I didn't want to accidentally kill him. A blow like that could also damage the instruments. Two: I could scream for help. But would anyone hear me? The walls were thick and the sweatshops below were closed. That left number three: I could attempt to communicate.

"What are you doing here?" I asked.

He erupted in a long, wheezing giggle. "*Heh-heh-heh.* Shouldn't I be asking you that question?" he said.

So. Option number three wasn't working. Petra should really start locking her door. New York City was dangerous.

"The magazine flew me back for a couple of days to load up on supplies," he said. "I couldn't find the kind of film I needed in Guatemala. I just thought I'd check up on the place and see how Petra was doing."

My jaw dropped. "You're her *dad*?" I gasped.

He giggled again. "Yeah, but don't worry. Black people make me nervous, too."

"I—no—jeez, I'm sorry," I stammered. The bass case slipped from my shoulder and hit the floor with a clumsy thud. "Petra didn't tell me you would be here—"

"Relax. She didn't know. It's cool." He flopped down on the couch. "So which one are you? Bartholomew?"

"Hen." I tried to smile, scrambling for the bass. Petra's guitar

fell off on top of it. I scooped both instruments up in my arms.
"I—I—"

"Ease up, chief!" He laughed again. "I'll be out of your way in a minute. I'm sleeping at my girlfriend's place. I was just hanging out. I lost track of the time."

I bit my lip. I had no idea what to say. He was right: The fact that he was black *had* made me nervous. I was a horrible human being.

"So how was the gig?" he asked. "Sorry I couldn't make it. Oh, wait, before I forget—one of Petra's friends dropped by and asked me to give her this." He held the letter toward me. "Would you mind passing it along?"

"No, no. Of course not." I left the instruments in a heap on the floor and shambled over to him. But as soon as I plucked the paper from his fingers, I froze. On the back was written: *For Petra*. I recognized the handwriting instantly. It was Emma's.

"Hey, are you sure you're okay, chief? You look a little pale." He chuckled. "You know, paler than most white people."

"I . . . um . . ." I forced an awkward laugh. My eyes darted between him and the note. If this was meant for Petra, I probably shouldn't read it. Then again, *he'd* been reading it when I walked in. Besides, Petra and Emma wouldn't even be friends if it weren't for me. It wasn't in an envelope. It might as well be public property.

"I always used to get the shakes after I played a gig, too," he said. He pulled a small wooden pipe out of his pocket and tucked it between his teeth, then grabbed a pack of matches from the coffee table. "Conventional wisdom says you're more nervous before you get onstage, but I say you're more nervous *after*. You're loaded with adrenaline. I played bass in a band, too—did Petra tell you? Roxy Mountain High. We were like the Meters meets the Allman Brothers . . ."

I stopped listening. I honestly hadn't meant to read whatever Emma had written to Petra—at least not right there and then, not right in front of him. But once I started, I couldn't stop.

Hey, Petra,

You're probably wondering why I took the time to give you the gift of a handwritten letter. I was going to send you a text or an email, but that just felt too 21st century. In deference to your hallowed nineties vibe, I am kicking it way, WAY old school. Feel free to frame this, in fact.

That was a joke. But enough of my stalling.

In all seriousness, I'm writing to say I'm sorry. And why, may you ask? Well, for starters, I am sorry for assuming the role of Hen's Yoko and hanging out uninvited with you guys these past few days. (What's the proper term? "Yoko Without Benefits"?) The reason I've been said YWB is even sillier than said term. I wanted to sabotage your gig.

Wow. Writing it down looks even more awful than saying it out loud.

But I had a good reason, I swear. See, I wanted Hen to feel okay about himself when you kicked him out of the band again. I wanted him to hate the band and the gig and, yes, maybe even you so badly that he'd breathe a huge sigh of relief when it was all over and ask himself: "Jeez, what was I even thinking playing bass for Dawson's Freak? Thank God I'm out."

Honestly, my plan made sense when I formulated it in my head. (I admit I'm a little wacko.) But the thing is, during my brief tenure as YWB I saw that you weren't just stringing him along. Unless you're evil incarnate, which I'm pretty sure you're not, you still really do want to be friends with him. You even helped take his mind off his sister. Which is a big thing. So you deserve props, whether you know it or not.

So if you can, please forgive me for being a jerk and pretending like Dawson's Freak sucks. Because you don't. You rocked tonight. I mean it. I'm sorry I cut out before it was over. I'm also sorry more people didn't come to the gig. They will next time, though. I'll friend a thousand people on Facebook and make sure of it. Well, okay, maybe closer to 900 . . . ☺

Hen was right all long. I never gave you the benefit of the doubt because you're so fa-boo, but you're a cool chick. You go, girl!

Ugh. I want to barf now.

Your friend (I hope),

Emma Wood

PS: I quit drinking. That was just part of the act.

My throat tightened. My eyes began to sting. I blinked several times. Suddenly I realized that the air had filled with pot smoke. I glanced up from the page.

Petra's dad sucked in his breath and held the pipe in my direction. "Want a hit?" he asked in a strained voice. He didn't exhale.

I peered at the glowing embers in the bowl. I'd never gotten stoned before, and I had a definite feeling it wouldn't be wise to make this my first time. "No thanks," I said.

He flashed me a used-car-salesman grin. "It's Guatemalan homegrown."

"No, really. I'm cool."

"So what was I saying?" He coughed. "Oh, right. Your band. No offense, chief, but I think if Petra really wants to make it big, she has to lose you guys. It's all about the solo acts these days. I'm sure you guys rock and all, but . . ."

I stopped listening. My eyes were still teary. I was overwhelmed by a sudden urge to rush back to Brooklyn and hug Emma as tightly as I could. She didn't have to write that letter. It would have been a lot easier for her to play Yoko Without Benefits until I *did* get kicked out of Dawson's Freak again. But Emma didn't operate that way. I was her friend. She was looking out for me, even if her plan *was* a little convoluted and hurtful. But that didn't even matter. The hurt was only for the good. *My* good. Besides, if she made a mistake, she copped to it. And she hadn't complimented Petra or the band or the show because she thought it would somehow get back to me, either.

There were no ulterior motives, other than being nice.

Amazing. I'd forgotten people like that existed in real life. If only the world were populated with clones of Emma Wood . . . Jesus. I'm normally not a walking cheese factory, but I couldn't help myself. "The Age of Aquarius" started blasting through my head. I finally understood what the song was about. If everyone were more like Emma, we'd all be jigging around together in blissful harmony, and the planet would be a sunny, Technicolor wonderland described in a thousand corny Grateful Dead songs. (Was "The Age of Aquarius" by the Grateful Dead? Whatever.) All would be paradise.

" . . . the thing is, you're not gonna get signed," Petra's dad was saying. He smiled, his eyes red slits. "I'm not saying that you're *never* gonna get signed, like in some different band down the road. But with your current lineup, things just aren't gonna happen. And it's not just that Petra needs to go solo. The era of the power trio is over . . .."

I nodded. I knew I should be offended, but he'd lost me. I couldn't get my mind off Emma. Once in a great while—when I was lonely or desperate or depressed (and, yes, I happened to be all three at the moment)—I would convince myself that we *should* have been a couple. Just like all the troglodytes wanted. Had I made some kind of egregious, catastrophic mistake by never making a move? We could have been hooking up ever since I'd "discovered girls." Practically married. I *could* have made out with her at the dog run. I *could* have made eye contact during the second song tonight. Yet somehow, somewhere, we'd slipped into permanent friends mode. Had that been a conscious decision on my part? It didn't seem likely. As far as I knew, Gabriel was absolutely right: I was always thinking about hooking up with any female, at any time.

"I should probably go," Petra's dad said.

"Huh?"

He giggled loudly. "Damn, chief, what have *you* been smoking?"

I shook my head and blinked, then folded the letter and clutched it tightly. "Sorry, I'm just . . ." I didn't finish.

"Make sure Petra gets that, all right? I think it's important." He stood and dumped the ashes on the floor, then tried to brush them aside with his Birkenstocks. "It's funny. I was just talking about power trios with some of the guys from Phish. You remember that band? Great live show."

I shook my head.

"Yeah, I know. Your thing is nineties rap rock, right?" He tucked the pipe back into his pocket. "Too bad. I mean, I get the joke, but Petra can do better than that."

"She probably can," I agreed quietly.

"Don't worry." Petra's dad patted me on the shoulder and shuffled to the door, leaving a trail of ash footprints. "When I was in high school, I was just like you. I wanted to be a rock star, too. But then I realized I had to practice." He burst out laughing, as if he were a rabid fan at his own stand-up comedy show. "Once you see how hard it is to make it, something else will pop up. It always does."

I shrugged and nodded.

"Yo, chief, I didn't mean to bum you out. I'm just talking out my ass. It's the jet lag. I was in London the day before yesterday. What's your name again? Ben?"

"Hen," I said.

"My fault, Hen. Take care, all right? And keep an eye on Petra. She's a crazy one." He paused. "Y'all aren't doing the nasty, are you?"

"Every night," I heard myself answer.

He burst out laughing again. "*Heh-heh-heh!* My man. Just be safe. Peace."

"Hey, wait! Can I ask you something?"

"Shoot."

I bit my lip. "Are you really friends with a friend of the guy who made the Steal Your Parents' Money stickers?"

His bloodshot eyes narrowed. "Probably. I know a lot of cats."

"Oh," I said. "Well. Just curious."

He nodded, looking vaguely concerned. "Get some rest, chief."

I watched as the front door slammed behind him.

For a moment, I just stood there. Whoa. The warm, snuggly Emma-is-a-goddess feeling quickly evaporated into thin air, like the pot smoke.

That bizarre little encounter had seriously unnerved me. On the one hand, I was certain that Petra's dad was a stoned, stuck-up idiot. Did he really believe that I was doing "the nasty" with his daughter? Did he really not care? And what was he even talking about? The era of the power trio was over? Then why did half the bands on MTV fit that description? Without thinking, I could probably name five: Green Day, and . . . *hmm*. All right, one. And they'd peaked in the nineties. But still. There hadn't been as many power trios gigging around New York since the days of Cream and the Jimi Hendrix Experience. If anything, I'd always assumed there were *too* many power trios.

On the other hand . . . *what*? He wasn't trying to be a jerk. Actually, he was a supermellow guy—considering that I'd probably come off as a racist.

Suddenly I realized what bothered me about him. He reminded me of Emma's dad. Seriously. He was the black stoner version. He handled himself with the same stupid jocularity. And he came at you with the same rude, nonstop, volume-on-eleven broadcast: *Look at me! Dig it! I'm a success and you're just a dumb teenager!*

But that was my problem, not his. He'd earned the right. He *deserved* to be a dick. I was just jealous. I may have been an "adult," but he was a grown-up brat, and he could get away with it. I wanted what he had, times a million. And like he said, I didn't want to have to practice bass a lot to get there, either.

Boy, was I insightful. Yes. Kudos for me.

That's the wonderful thing about being so miserable: It allows you to see your faults with perfect clarity and still feel detached enough to be okay with them.

I dropped Emma's letter on the coffee table. Then I picked up my bass and left.

You want to know what's *really* funny? Even after all that, I still wished that my dad were more like him and Emma's dad. I really did.

CHAPTER FIFTEEN
Rumpelstiltskins, All of Them

"Dude!"

Somebody was pounding on my bedroom door.

"Dude!"

I blinked several times. *Petra?*

"Wake up, already!"

It *was* Petra. But she never showed up at my place unannounced. And she never used the word "dude" unless something wonderful or miraculous had happened.

"HEN!"

"Coming," I croaked. My skull was pounding. Sometime since I'd last been conscious, Petra's voice had acquired the destructive force of a jackhammer. I lurched out of bed, squinting in the sunlight. The blinds were drawn, but they didn't help. I really needed some curtains in here. Heavy, black, velvet curtains. That, and a vat of industrial-strength aspirin.

"You're not gonna believe this," she said as I threw open the door.

"I . . . what?"

She scurried past me and hit the eject button on my stereo, then dug into her bag and yanked out a loose CD. "We were up until four, tweaking it," she murmured excitedly. "I haven't even slept . . ." She dropped in the CD and pressed play. Nothing happened. She stomped her foot on the floor. My brain vibrated in painful sympathy. Ouch. I should have worn earplugs last night. If we played any more gigs, I'd be deaf before I was twenty-one. Either that or have a permanent migraine.

"Listen," she whispered.

The next instant, my walls were shaking with what sounded like a Parliament Funkadelic outtake. My head spun. I grabbed the doorframe to steady myself. She turned the volume all the way up. It was loud enough to drown out my creaking joints, my rumbling empty belly—even the traffic outside.

"What are you *doing*?" I shouted.

She raised a finger to her lips. I glared at her. She smiled back. Her eyes were puffy. Suddenly I realized she was wearing the same black cocktail dress she had worn at the gig. In the glare of the sunrays, her outfit had a shimmering, hallucinatory quality. I wouldn't be surprised if her dad had secretly drugged me when he'd patted my shoulder last night and sent me off on a very, very bad time-delayed trip. Didn't a famous Beat

Generation novelist once compare a bad headache to the more sinister effects of psychedelics? I thought I remembered reading that in a book Sarah had once lent me . . .

"He's gonna tu-r-r-rn his mu-tha out," a silky female falsetto sang. "He's gonna turn his mutha . . . OUT."

My mouth fell open.

"Oedipus Wrecks." It wasn't Parliament Funkadelic. It was *us*.

We were unrecognizable. Petra sounded like Mary J. Blige. The bass had a crisp bite. I could hear every note. The instruments were all distinct, but the different layers blended perfectly—the fuzz of the guitar, the click of the hi-hat, the pounding bottom . . . . This couldn't have been recorded last night. No way. I shook my head as the song bounced to its climax. There was a measure of tight, razor-sharp quarter notes: *chink, chink, chink, chink*—then *crash!*—it was over, followed by applause.

More than three people were clapping. A lot more.

She turned down the volume knob. "I pasted in a sample of some crowd noise," she said with a proud grin.

I shook my head in awe. "I don't get it," I whispered. "How did you do it?"

"Bartholomew has a special effects sampler. It's part of the ACID Pro package. It's got a laugh track and boos and a bunch of other—"

"No, no," I interrupted. "How did you fix the recording? How did you make us sound so good?"

Petra couldn't stop smiling. "It's that software Bartholomew

186

has, that stuff he's been telling you about! He showed me how it works last night. But we played much better than I thought, anyway. Rehearsing every day helps. The gig was really tight. Your bass playing killed, too, sweetie." She smirked. "Well, up until your string broke."

"I had no idea," I said. My headache evaporated. I'd never loved Bartholomew Savage more than at that moment. I wanted to plant a sloppy kiss right smack on his handsome face. He was a genius. No wonder horrible live bands sounded so good in the studio. There was nothing a gifted sound engineer couldn't do. Absolutely nothing. They were Rumpelstiltskins, all of them. They could take straw and spin it into gold.

My cell phone started ringing. It was still in my pants' pocket, in a pile on the floor. I fished the phone out with one hand and yanked the corduroys over my boxers with the other, eyeing the caller ID. Sweet. It was Bartholomew Savage.

"Hey!" I said excitedly. "What's up? This is karma! Petra is playing me our demo right now. Thank you so much! You gotta come over and—"

"Hen?" He sounded annoyed.

"Yeah?"

"I can't play with you guys anymore."

The words floated right by me. I must not have heard him correctly. I was too giddy. "What was that?" I said.

"I quit."

My grip tightened around the phone. I glanced over at Petra. She furrowed her brow.

"I'm sorry, you *what*?"

"You really made me look like an asshole last night," Bartholomew Savage said.

I swallowed. "Wait. I don't—"

"Sid just called. I can't believe you told him to screw himself. He did *us* a favor. I have to go back there and pay him myself. You owe me sixty bucks, by the way. Sid is really pissed at my brother. Irene is pissed, too, with all the wackness you talked. Victor might lose his job. I hope you're happy."

My stomach twisted. Good God. I had no idea what to say. Had I behaved *that* badly? What "wackness" had I talked? And who was Irene?

"What's going on?" Petra hissed.

I waved her off. "Look, I'm really sorry," I murmured urgently. "Why don't you give me Sid's number and let me call him to explain—"

"Forget it," Bartholomew Savage interrupted. "Just come over and bring sixty bucks. Or give it to Petra. She can give it to me."

There was a loud click. I flinched.

"Hello? Hello?"

"Is that Bartholomew?" Petra demanded.

I stared at the phone. My jaw hung slack. The line was dead. He'd hung up.

"Well?" she pressed.

"It *was*," I muttered. I shoved the phone back into my pocket.

"What did he want? What's going on?"

"I don't know," I said. I sat down on the edge of the bed and ran a hand through my hair. "I think he just quit the band."

"He just quit the band," she repeated.

I nodded. I felt sick.

"Why would he do that?" she asked. Her voice was oddly colorless.

"I . . . uh, I think it has something to do with Sid, the guy who made the recording. And somebody named Irene."

"Somebody named Irene," she said.

Our gazes locked. Her face darkened. "Loser" played softly on the stereo. Luckily, the song had just begun. My D string wouldn't break for several minutes. I opened my mouth to apologize—but the door swung open and Dad walked in.

"Sorry to interrupt," he said. "I wanted to see what all the ruckus was about."

Petra and I kept staring at each other. Both of us were breathing heavily. The song had reached the guitar solo: the best part, maybe even the highlight of our set. Petra copied the melody of the chorus in Biggie Smalls' "Hypnotize," the part where the female voices sing "Biggie, Biggie, Biggie, can't you see?" She played the riff note for note, only with heavy delay, so it sounded as if three guitarists were playing together in the back of a cathedral. The effect was incredible, very trippy. My expression softened.

Petra reached over and snapped the power off.

"What music is that?" Dad asked.

"It's . . . um, our band," I muttered.

"Really?" He sounded surprised. "*Your* band?"

"Yeah. We made a recording of our gig last night."

He smiled. "Well. I'm very impressed. I'd love to hear the whole thing at some point. Please don't blast it so loudly, though. I'm working at home today. I'm sure the Wood family got a sampling of it. The whole block did."

My mood abruptly screeched around in a 180-degree turn. Ha! I flashed Petra a triumphant smile. The situation wasn't so dire, after all. If *Dad* said he liked it, then it *was* probably worthy of immediate release on a major label. It was the first time he'd ever complimented anything musical I'd ever done.

"What are you doing here, anyway, Hen?" Dad asked.

I laughed. "I live here, remember?"

"So you really liked it?" Petra asked him, ignoring his bizarre question. Her tone was suspicious.

The phone rang again before he could answer. My heart jumped. I didn't recognize the number. Maybe Bartholomew Savage was calling from a different line and had changed his mind.

"Hello?" I answered breathlessly.

"Is that Hen?"

I blinked. It was Mrs. Abrahmson. She'd never called me before.

"Hi," I said.

"Do you plan on walking the dogs today? Or can't you be bothered?"

Uh-oh. I glanced around the room. My eyes zeroed in on the digital clock on the stereo. 11:51. My heart thumped. I should have been at her place over three hours ago. I was already late for the *second* walk. I'd forgotten it was Thursday. I had just assumed it was a Sunday, because last night felt like a Saturday.

"Wow, I'm really sorry—"

"If I were smart, I'd say that you should look for another job," she remarked, "but I rather like you, Hen Birnbaum. I assume you had a gig last night?"

Okay. Maybe Petra's father *had* drugged me. Nothing made sense. Dad was being kind about my music, and Mrs. Abrahmson suddenly knew I was in a band. I'd never once mentioned Dawson's Freak to her. At least I thought I hadn't. We hardly ever spoke. She was usually on her iPhone for those three seconds when she opened her door and handed me the leashes.

"You are a musician, right?" she asked.

"Well, yeah. But I—"

"I can spot them a mile away, you know. My husband tries to be a musician when he isn't practicing law. I play a little tambourine, myself. We're obsessed with the classics. Why do you think we named our dogs after John Bonham and John Entwistle?"

Bonzo and Ox.

The names suddenly clicked. Bonzo: the nickname John Bonham's friends and band mates gave him. "The Ox": the moniker the Who's bassist, John Entwistle, had given himself (why, I don't know).

My God. I never would have made that connection. Glenda Abrahmson wasn't supposed to know the aliases of classic rock icons. She wasn't supposed to be cool. She was supposed to be an eccentric, overpampered nightmare. But now . . .

Incredible. The Unseen Hand was poised for a high-five.

All at once, anything seemed possible. Emma's father *could* get us a recording contract. Why the hell not? And so what if I'd talked "wackness" in front of Sid and Irene, whoever she was? (Aha: the sour bartender.) That was my prerogative. I'd happily pay the sixty bucks I owed Sid now, too. Besides, I bet Bartholomew Savage would come crawling back to Dawson's Freak once Emma's father was on board. Even if he didn't, we'd find another drummer in no time. The label could find us a drummer, for God's sake.

"Ah, the price of age," Glenda Abrahmson said with a wistful sigh. "I suppose you're too young to remember Zeppelin or the Who. Or I'm too old to talk about them. Bloody hell. Better not get me started. Are you coming over, then?"

It took me less than fifteen minutes to get to Thomas Street by cab. There was hardly any traffic. I hummed the Who's "My Generation" to myself the whole way. A glorious new phase of my summer employment was about to begin. Mrs. Abrahmson would finally invite me inside the hallowed sanctuary of her apartment. She would show me her tambourine, and we would analyze her husband's best Zep bootlegs. . . .

But none of that happened.

Mrs. Abrahmson simply opened the door—iPhone against her cheek—handed over the dogs, and shut me back out with a smirk, as if to say, *Don't screw up again.*

That was it.

When I got to the dog run, Emma was nowhere to be seen, either.

I sat down on the bench and checked my watch. It was a little past 12:30.

The dogs settled into a heap at my feet and abruptly began to snore. I peered into the brown paper bag my mom had handed me on the way out the door: a tuna sandwich, soy chips, and a Poland Spring.

I should have been hungry. I hadn't eaten yet. I should have been a lot of things: worried, freaked out, sorrowful, upset, bothered, angry, curious. But I was none of the above. I was an empty glass. Even my old pal Jim Forbes had disappeared. Maybe there was nothing left to say.

CHAPTER SIXTEEN
It's a Joke of a Life

My mood only got progressively stranger, my metaphorical glass as empty as could be, until I shambled home from the midday dog walk.

Then, well . . . everything changed.

Emma was in my bed. When I trudged up the stairs and opened my bedroom door, I found her there—stretched leisurely out on top of the covers, barefoot, in a flowery spaghetti-strap sundress. Her head was propped up against my pillows . . . and what do you think she was doing? Well, well, well. That Emma Wood. Reading my stolen copy of *Diary of My Life on the Lam*, by Gabriel Stern.

She glanced up from the pages.

Neither of us spoke.

"I read the whole thing," she blurted out.

For whatever reason, that lit the fuse. Ka-boom. It wasn't just a laugh attack. It was a breakdown. It *hurt*. I understood what the term "sidesplitting" meant now. It came in waves. Just when I thought I was getting a grip, I'd look at her lying there, and the hysterics would start all over again. We must have laughed for two straight minutes.

"Good lord," she gasped once it was over. "Listen, Hen, let's make a pact, all right? Let's not talk about this diary right now." She tossed it onto my nightstand. It bounced off the clock radio and fell to the floor, facedown.

A final giggle escaped my lips. I nodded and took another deep breath. "Deal."

She heaved a shaky sigh of relief. "Good man."

"Emma, do you think I've changed since Sarah came back and disappeared again?" I asked suddenly. That wasn't how I planned on starting a new conversation. But the question popped out of my mouth, so we were forced to work with it.

"Why? Did your dad say something? He told me I should come up here and make myself at home."

I shook my head. "No, no. It's just . . ."

"That's what's bothering you?" Emma asked.

"Actually, what's really bothering me is that Bartholomew Savage quit our band."

She looked puzzled. "Because you've changed?"

"Among other reasons, I guess," I muttered.

"Oh, well. That's too bad. He's cute."

I pursed my lips, annoyed. We weren't here to discuss Bartholomew Savage's effect on Emma's libido. This was my room. If she was going to invite herself in and read my stolen merchandise without permission, then she was not allowed to talk about anybody who was cooler, younger, and better looking than me.

"Don't worry," she said. "I'm sure he'll change his mind. You just got unlucky with the crowd last night. If they'd let all his friends in, he wouldn't be so upset. You guys sounded amazing. That's the important thing. Really."

"Thanks." Maybe she was right. Only now I wasn't so sure that Bartholomew Savage would return. And we needed him back. No label would ever sign a bass and guitar duo, would they? Of course not. I hadn't been thinking straight. I'd just been high on the recording. Finding a replacement would be impossible. Drummers in New York were like cabdrivers: only one out of every hundred was competent, English speaking, or drug free. We couldn't afford to lose him.

"Have a seat, Hen," Emma said gently, slapping the mattress.

I crawled onto the bed and stretched out beside her, staring at the ceiling.

She nudged me with her elbow. "Come on. What's really bothering you?"

I lifted my shoulders a little but was thinking: Nothing ever works out the way I see it in my head. Mrs. Abrahmson had slammed the door in my face yet again. Our drummer hated my guts. Petra would kick me out of the band way before she kicked out Bartholomew Savage. She'd probably kick me out today, in fact. Anxiety crept over me; I felt a sudden compulsion to give our demo to Emma's dad today, this afternoon, *now*.

But why? Did I really, truly believe deep down that he could get Dawson's Freak a recording contract? For the past few weeks, I'd based every move I'd made on the absurd premise that becoming a rock star would bring Sarah back and make my family normal again (or close enough). It wasn't laughable—it was psychotic. I was slipping deeper and deeper into the abyss, and I knew it.

"Can I tell you something?" Emma murmured. "When I left the dog run yesterday, I noticed another dog walker on her way in—a girl with a bunch of little puppies. She was our age, kind of an indie-rock chick, and she had a Steal Your Parents' Money pin on her hat. I was thinking: What's her story? Is she in a band, too? Is she a wannabe artist? A fauxhemian? Is she writing a memoir about how *she's* the actual unsung mystery genius behind that slogan?"

"Everybody's the actual unsung mystery genius behind that slogan," I mumbled.

"I *know*. But it's like, everybody wants to be famous—but nobody has that thing that is gonna push them over the top . . . that aura, that drive, whatever. And when I saw you guys last night—even though nobody was there, even though you might not have been happy with how it went—I just saw that you had it. And this girl didn't. I could just tell. Don't ask me how. But something big will happen to you sooner or later, Hen. I'm not just saying that. I'm not being sarcastic, either. I haven't had a single beer. I really believe it."

I tried to muster a smile. I felt like crying all of a sudden. Emma was a bottomless pit of goodwill. How could she volunteer at a homeless shelter—a job she'd gotten solely for my benefit, no less—deal with her insane father, listen to my messed-up ramblings . . . and still manage to be so *sweet*?

"I didn't say it was going to be easy," she teased.

"I know," I said. "But it's funny. Something weird happened to me just now. Mrs. Abrahmson told me that she named her dogs after members of Led Zeppelin and the Who. Mrs. *Abrahmson*. And I was, like, whoa—this is a sign, an omen that amazing things are on the horizon, that there's this connection, that my family will finally tell me—" I stopped midsentence. I didn't even know what I was trying to say.

Emma laughed. "You think that's something new?"

"What do you mean?"

"Hen, you see signs and omens in everything. That's the way you are."

"Is that bad?" I asked nervously.

"It's cute."

I wasn't sure if I liked that adjective. It was the second time she'd used it.

She patted my knee. "You see these connections, and you believe in them, and that's what makes them real."

Her fingers stayed put. I watched them there, comfortably

nestled in the folds of my corduroys.

My thoughts drifted, billowed by Emma's closeness. I thought about that letter she'd written Petra. I thought about *Hen Birnbaum's Super-Awesome Nineties Nostalgia Mix!!!* I thought about how she'd found the stolen manuscript because she knew exactly where to look, and how she was sure we'd have a blast going to that stupid Journey concert with her parents, because we would. "The Age of Aquarius" hummed quietly in my brain.

I tilted my head slightly. Her eyes were closed. A soft, inviting smile played on her lips.

That dress!

My pulse quickened. Was it? Yes . . . it was. The same dress from my dream. My God. Was the Unseen Hand tapping my shoulder? It had to be.

There *was* a connection between reality and my dream life. This was real. Nothing had ever felt *more* real. Here we were, alone in my room, side by side on my bed, joined together. . . . Gabriel was right.

Indescribable warmth washed over me.

Gabriel was right.

I felt it: that 100 percent certainty he knew I'd have if we'd made eye contact while I was onstage. Only now there was no wall of make-believe between us. Her eyes were closed, but that was even better. I wanted to kiss her. I *had* to. She was waiting for it; I could tell. That smile! It was no accident, either. We'd only joked with the troglodytes to mask the truth. It was destiny. I needed to forget about all the crap in my life—not only everything that was going on with Sarah and my parents and Petra and the band . . . I needed to forget every preconceived notion I ever had about Emma.

Now was the time. This moment. *Now*, before it got too late or too weird or impossible, just like Gabriel said it would. She wanted me to.

Look at her lying there, waiting! She's my best friend . . .

I leaned over. I closed my eyes. My lips pressed softly against hers. They melted against mine. She kissed me back—

"Hen, stop," she breathed.

My heart galloped. I could barely hear her.

"Stop." She pulled away. "Stop. Stop."

And then it was over. Just like that.

The kiss lasted five seconds, ten at most. No time at all. But it was enough. CAUTION: POLICE LINE—DO NOT CROSS. I'd done it. I'd broken the tape, the seal protecting the one taboo that had been alluded to and avoided and joked about and danced around for our entire lives. Today. Here. *Now*.

The problem was, Emma did something I never, ever imagined she would do.

She started sobbing.

No, no, no. This was all wrong.

Tears streamed down her cheeks. Her lips were trembling. It wasn't supposed to happen this way. Who was I kidding? I hadn't just imagined this exact scenario in a few dreams; I envisioned it a thousand times *awake*. Really, if I were honest with myself, I thought about it almost every day; I just buried it on autopilot. And it was always perfect. It always transcended any comparison with a scene from a book or a film or a song I'd enshrined in my private pantheon—because it was *better*, something timeless, something (if a comparison had to be made) along the lines of Jimmy Stewart smooching with Donna Reed in *It's a Wonderful Life*.

So what was going on? Frank Capra would not approve. But then, this was another movie entirely: *It's a Joke of a Life*, starring Henry Birnbaum—written, directed, and produced by the same.

"Emma, I'm so sorry," I whispered.

She shook her head and sniffed, clumsily scooting to the foot of the bed.

"Don't worry," she said, her voice quavering.

"Emma, I didn't mean—"

"No, no, no, I'm just confused," she cut in. "That's all. It's Gabriel's diary. It's everything. I get so bugged out and I don't even know—"

"No, no, it's my fault!" I cried. "I had this dream. I mean . . ." I hesitated, teetering on the brink of saying: *I don't even like you that way.* But that was worse than a dopey, pitiful lie; it was *evil*. I was just looking for an excuse: anything to take back what I'd done, anything to erase the moment. What was I *thinking*? Emma wasn't *attracted* to me! Dreams or no dreams, there was no destiny involved. She put her hand on my knee because she's my *best friend*. At most, she'd been making a joke. A joke!

201

I'd never felt more disgusting. I was covered in slime. I'd forced my sloppy lips on hers—upon the lips of Emma Wood, my neighbor, my pal, my sort-of sister! *Eww.* Forget shame, forget travesty, forget apocalypse . . . there isn't a word for it. If the Unseen Hand *were* present, it was giving me the finger.

"It's not you, Hen." Emma sniffled, avoiding my eyes. "It's me. Really. I always cry for no reason when I'm confused." She wiped her nose and glanced back at me, trying to smile. "Nothing happened."

My mouth opened, but no words would come. *Nothing happened?* Did she really mean that? And the worst part: She'd used the same moronic cliché that she ridiculed the night Petra broke up with me. "It's not you; it's me." The excuse that belonged in heinous pop songs written by fools. Meaningless. Beyond meaningless.

She bolted for the door.

"Emma, wait!" I shouted.

"Nothing happened!" she called back, scrambling down the stairs. Her footsteps echoed through the house, faster and faster—

Before I could shout her name again, the front door slammed.

PART III

The Surprise Twist That I Probably Should Have Seen Coming

CHAPTER SEVENTEEN
Perfect Timing

Didn't I say I was entitled to a little self-pity every now and then? Good. Now how about a little *Behind the Music* style melodrama to go with it?

Jim Forbes, take it away. (Cue deafening orchestral soundtrack here) *"Hen Birnbaum: A walking tragedy. A cripple, to whom the bully's rule of the playground no longer applied. The proverbial arm had been hacked off. Only a bloody stump remained for that day and that long, long night: a fitting tribute to the Emma kiss-but-not-a-kiss. Forget rap rock bottom. Not even I, Jim Forbes himself, could do the poor wretch any justice."*

There you have it.

Some details: I couldn't sleep (big shocker). I told Mom and Dad I had the stomach flu, and then switched the diagnosis to food poisoning (grosser and more incapacitating, so they'd leave me alone). I emailed Mrs. Abrahmson to say that I couldn't walk or feed her dogs anymore (good riddance). I left Gabriel a voice mail letting him know I was taking a break from bass lessons (at midnight, when I knew he'd be asleep). I sat at my computer in a daze, waiting for Emma to email or text or call. (She didn't.) I left only to use the bathroom.

Saddest of all, somehow: Mom placed a little bowl of plain rice and a thermos of ginger ale outside my door, along with a note:

> *Stay hydrated. And please, please put your dirty clothes in the hamper if you feel up to it. Love you, Mom.*

Tragic, right? And the kicker—
Sarah updated her Facebook news feed again.

Sarah Birnbaum is doing her happy dance.
Sarah Birnbaum can't wait to get back to her gardening.
Sarah Birnbaum is thrilled that her friend Karl decided to buy a second home.
Sarah Birnbaum is equally thrilled that Karl and Madeline are coming to New York City to visit.
Sarah Birnbaum is grateful that **Henry** has been wonderful enough not to mention any of this to Mom and Dad. She'll thank him with a big hug tomorrow.
Sarah Birnbaum is now friends with **Rich Hussein Barry** and **Tony Cox**

Sarah Birnbaum promises to visit **Rich Hussein Barry**
and **Tony Cox** in LA as soon as she saves enough money.

Amazing stuff. The prodigal daughter, on her way home
again. Just in time to witness how my joke of a life had finally
gone kaput.

And I *still* didn't know why she'd disappeared and come
back and disappeared again.

But, at the very least, I had a hunch she'd tell me now. She'd
settled whatever mysterious business needed settling. She'd
gone public with herself again. She wouldn't have friended
those guys Tony and Rich if she still had something to hide.
Mom and Dad were off the hook.

I checked out the Facebook profiles of Tony and Rich on
the off chance that *they* could put the final pieces of the puzzle
in place. But like Sarah, they hadn't uploaded any photos or
filled in any vital stats. They were nonentities. Blank pages.
Facebook friends in the truest sense: All they offered was connection itself. With whom or with what was anybody's guess.

Oh, and I almost forgot: at some point during the long
miserable night, Petra sent me an email, too.

Hey, sweetie,
Sorry I got so pissed at you this morning. I was just
stressed. So you know, I straightened everything out with
Bartholomew. Don't worry. He's still in the band. I paid Sid
the $60 myself and apologized for you. Victor isn't getting
fired. I don't know if the Bimbo Lounge will invite us back

anytime soon, but their loss, right? ☺

BTW, Bartholomew wants to change our name back to PETRA. He thinks it's stupid to label ourselves as a nineties nostalgia band. It's too limiting. I sort of agree. We're more than that. What do you think?

Also . . . there's been something I've been meaning to tell you. It's been bumming me out all summer. I should probably tell you in person, but I've been blowing it off because I feel so guilty about it. Argh.

I hooked up with George Monroe the night I broke up with you.

I'm sorry. I don't know what our deal will be when he gets back, but whatever happens, I want you to know: You're still in the band if you want to be.

You should know, too, Hen: I didn't break up with you because you aren't a good enough bass player. I broke up with you because you were never all that into me. I think you tried to pretend like you were for my sake, because you're such a sweetie, but you could never fake it in front of Emma.

She's totally in love with you. You know that, right?

xoxo Petra

Wow. Heavy, huh? Part of it made me smile. (George Monroe, you sly dog! I *did* deserve a gold star.) Most of it made me want to pull a Sarah Birnbaum and disappear for a long, long time— maybe never to return. The band could survive without me.

(Their loss, but . . .) If only Petra knew the truth about Emma. It might have even been funny, if it weren't.

At ten in the morning, there was a knock on my door.

"I'm still sleeping, Mom," I croaked.

"It's Emma."

The room turned upside down, dumping me out of bed.

I had a hard time with the doorknob. I kept fumbling with it and nearly knocked myself over when I finally yanked it open. My head spun. *Emma*—

There she stood.

Dark circles ringed her eyes. Her face was pale, almost snow-white. She probably hadn't slept, either. She was still wearing the same dress. Her hair looked like a bomb had gone off. She was beautiful.

I opened my mouth. "I—"

She grabbed me and kissed me.

It was more of a lunge. Practically violent. She squeezed her eyes shut. (I knew because mine were wide open.) Then she stepped back.

"Do you know how many times I've dreamed of doing that?" she asked hoarsely.

I stood motionless, still scared. "Really?"

"Not just in regular dreams. In everyday daydreams."

I swallowed. "Since when?"

Her eyes began to water. She sniffed and rubbed them, grimacing. "Since forever. Since we used to play hopscotch." Her voice was thick. "Look, do me a favor, okay? Pretend I didn't just fly to Palm Springs for tear duct surgery. The constant waterworks make me feel self-conscious. You can make fun of the Botox, but that's it."

Slowly, slowly—in spite of how hard I tried to cling to the shell I'd spent the last twenty hours tightening around myself—the fear that I'd lost Emma for good melted away. "You have a deal," I said, fighting to make my voice as dry as possible. "Didn't I tell you this face-lift was a risk?"

"I know. They made it seem so easy on *Nip/Tuck*. I should have paid more attention to the botched cases." She stared me straight in the eye, batting her wet eyelashes. "Hen, listen. I know you think that becoming a rock star is a stupid fantasy. But it isn't. You have to swear it isn't."

I shook my head, at a loss.

"Because I have a stupid fantasy, too," she went on. "A stupid, ridiculous, girly fantasy. I've had it ever since I moved next door to you. It's one of the few things I've never told you. You want to hear what it is?"

The golf ball in my throat made it impossible to speak.

"My dad springs for a huge outdoor wedding. It's a gorgeous summer day, like today. We close off the street, and he gets one of the lame bands he represents to play, and you and I take our vows right on my front stoop. What do you think of that?"

I nodded lamely. I didn't even know if that was the right response.

"See, if you pretend that your rock star fantasy isn't stupid, then I can pretend like my wedding fantasy isn't stupid, either. I can salvage some dignity. And I promise I'll never, ever run out on you again like I did yesterday. See, *I* was always supposed to make the first move. That was part of my fantasy, too. But I was never able to muster the courage. I was too scared you'd say no."

I extended a hand. "I'm saying yes," I choked out. "And you have a deal."

She shook it. Her hand was warm. She didn't let go.

I swept her into a very tight hug.

"I wonder if this is gonna make things easier or harder at school this fall," she whispered in my ear. "You know, with the troglodytes."

"Are you kidding?" I breathed. "Much easier. This will *really* confuse them."

If this were a normal story, that would be a perfect place to end.

Boy makes good with girl next door. Weirdness: over. New phase of relationship: on. A quick montage of bloopers and out-takes as the credits roll. Oh, the hilarity. Oh, the romance of it all. (No, we didn't *shtup*, if that's what you're wondering. What is this, porn? The morning was too pure and wondrous to be cheapened by gratuitous sex. We're saving that for later.) Cheers to us. Hooray for wholesome, predictable teen cheese.

Unfortunately, having a felon for a sister tends to ruin the possibility for a neat wrap-up. Okay, maybe that's overstating it. And, in fairness to Sarah, I wasn't sure if the label "felon" fit. Close enough, though. Actually, it's amazing how certain disaster areas of your life can seem a lot less complicated when the important stuff is taken care of. I shared this remarkable insight with Emma, and she agreed.

"She's really coming home today, huh?" Emma asked. We were lying in a comfy tangle on my bed. "You honestly think she's gonna spill the beans about everything?"

"I don't know. It seems that way."

"Well, it would be nice if she showed up sooner rather than later." She glanced at her watch. "It's almost noon. At five o'clock, you're mine."

I blushed slightly. "Oh, yeah? Why's that?"

"Please don't tell me you forgot about the Journey concert, Hen. Please."

"Holy crap." I sat up straight and ran a hand through my hair. "That's *tonight*, isn't it? I told my parents I'm sick. They think I'm at death's door."

"Well, you'll just have to convince them otherwise. My parents made reservations for the four of us at some swanky steak joint for an early dinner before the concert. Leave it to my dad to be sensitive about your vegetarianism."

I nodded. "Okay. I need to think. You know . . . it might be best if I sidestepped my family altogether and snuck out. We can climb down the fire escape. Besides, running away seems to be great reverse psychology with them. Sarah ran away, and they do everything she wants. Maybe they'll do everything *I* want now."

She wriggled her eyebrows. "You naughty boy! I like your thinking. Where to? My place? Conveniently, it's close by."

My gaze fell to Gabriel's manuscript, still facedown on the floor. "No. This'll sound insane, but what do you say we go to Gabriel's?"

Emma's eyes widened. "You mean now?"

"Yeah. Right now. You and me. Together. To come clean."

"Come clean about *what*?"

"To tell him that I *did* steal one of his manuscripts. And to tell him that he was right. See . . . he knew about us."

She squeezed my hand. "He did, huh? What did you tell him?"

"I don't even know. It was sort of like he read my mind."

"And you really want to tell him you lifted one of his manuscripts? You're a brave man, Hen. A total wack-a-doodle, but brave." She let out a deep, contented sigh. "Well, count me in. I'm sort of dying to see what he looks like, anyway."

As far as supernatural coincidences go, the timing worked out perfectly. I swear; I wasn't even all that surprised. The subway ride and stroll through the East Village put the two of us at Gabriel's apartment building at the same moment a taxicab pulled up to the curb—and out climbed you know who.

"Hey, Sarah," Emma said brightly.

She stared at us as the cab sped off. A faint smile curled her lips. She was as tan and stylish as ever, dolled up in sandals, a wide-brimmed white sunhat, and a silky, pricey-looking aquamarine dress. (Since when had she started caring so much about her wardrobe?) With her little Samsonite luggage on wheels, she looked as if she could have come straight from the set of some glamorous tropical fashion shoot. Wow. That Sarah Birnbaum. She really knew how to live life on the run, didn't she?

Her eyes narrowed.

"What?" I asked her.

"Why is Emma's hand in your back pocket?"

Jesus. Emma wrenched it free. I hadn't even realized it was there. I guess we'd been doing that corny new-couple snuggle walk since we'd exited the subway . . . I turned to Emma. Her cheeks looked as pink as mine felt. The Unseen Hand, I thought, and almost laughed.

"Did I miss something while I was away?" Sarah asked.

Neither Emma nor I said a word. We both lifted our shoulders.

Sarah smirked. "Never mind. I can probably figure it out. Man, you disappear for a couple of weeks, and everyone starts falling for each other. It's a good thing I'll be staying put."

"Really?" I asked. "You're really staying put?"

"I really am," she said. "Look, Hen . . . I'm so, so sorry I put you through all this. But I can tell you everything now. I just sold our house in Puerto Plata. I even turned a profit, if you can believe it. I got all the money back to repay Gabriel's father."

My nose wrinkled. Repay Gabriel's father? I opened my mouth, but Emma raised a finger to my lips.

"Shh. Whaddya say we go inside, Sarah? You can tell us all about it."

CHAPTER EIGHTEEN
Steal Your Parents' Money

About the surprise twist that I probably should have seen coming . . .

Gabriel almost seemed to be expecting us. I mean, as a package. He shook hands with Emma as if he'd known her his entire life and kissed my sister on the lips the way Petra had kissed me the day of my audition, with just a little too much *fuego*. Then we stood there for about five minutes in his sterile little apartment, grinning at one another with weird, anticipatory looks.

Finally Sarah told Gabriel to tell Emma and me the whole story. "Right up until we ran away," she said. "You know, so Hen gets it."

It went like this.

For most of his life, Gabriel Stern had one parent. His mom died of cancer when he was a toddler. His dad, Roger Stern, never quite recovered from her death. This isn't to say that he retreated into a sad shell, writing unpublished poetry to his long-lost love. No, he reacted by becoming a colossal dick—one that made Emma's dad and Petra's dad look like kindhearted heroes by comparison. He turned into a degenerate gambler. He started going on sex tours to Cambodia and Thailand. He left Gabriel to the care of babysitters and nannies, even on holidays. But he was also a dazzling success. He quit his job as an investment banker and founded a hedge fund in 2002. In Gabriel's senior year of high school, his dad made over a hundred million dollars. The two of them moved into a penthouse apartment on Madison Avenue, whereupon Gabriel's dad gave Gabriel his own wing with a separate entrance, so they could avoid running into each other.

Now, none of this may sound especially tragic. Sad and pitiable, yes. But not a dire recipe for disaster. The real trouble, however, started when Gabriel started applying to colleges.

"I was rejected from every single college I applied to," he told us all. "Can you imagine? Picture yourself surrounded by jubilant schmucks who are all getting into the colleges of their dreams. I bet it's like how lepers must have felt in ancient Rome. There were six: Columbia, Vassar, Tufts, Haverford, George Washington University—and my safety, Boston College. *Safety.* Ha! What a great word. A euphemism for 'a lousy college even a dope like *you* could get into.'

"Columbia was the real disgrace, though. Dad was a Columbia alum. He and Mom met and fell in love at Columbia. They joined the student government together. They protested all the issues worth protesting. Gas lines? The CIA in Chile? Whatever was wrong during the late seventies—a very lame decade, even lamer than the one we've got going now. They drank and chain-smoked at all the right bars and cafés. They both graduated cum laude. To them, Columbia wasn't a college; it was a *chrysalis*. They came in like pupae. They went out like butterflies. Two beautiful, brilliant creatures flapping among the rest of us lowly insects, stinking of cigarette smoke.

"Afterward, they donated a few thousand bucks to the school.

"And *still*, I was rejected.

"Dad couldn't believe it. He called the admissions office in an outrage, demanding an explanation. How could his only child, his *scion*, be rejected? How on earth was this possible? 'Not enough extracurricular activities,' he was told. Apparently, playing bass in a self-made student band didn't count.

"The subtext was clear: I was lazy. And laziness is not an acceptable character flaw, as far as Dad is concerned. You can smoke, you can be neglectful, you can go on sex tours, you can make your only child feel like garbage . . . but if you're lazy? No. It won't do. So after that, he donated in the high five figures and secured my admission. I had to meet personally with the dean of students and director of admissions.

"After I started Columbia, I got over it, though. I tried not to let myself get angry with him over his frustration with me. I understood it. I *was* an unmotivated deadbeat.

"But then came the straw that broke the camel's back. I told him that I wanted to get a master's degree in religion. You know what he said? I had 'the foresight of an amoeba.' Those were his actual words. When I told him to go easy on me, he said: 'I'm your father, Gabriel, I'm not your friend.' He finished by telling me that if I went to graduate school for religion, I'd have to pay for it myself. It was business school or nothing. He was cutting me off. Disowning me. And that's exactly what he did."

I flinched. Whoa.

Gabriel took a deep breath. His eyes were moist. I glanced at Emma. She blinked uncomfortably.

My sister took off her sun hat and clasped it in front of her.

"Did you know that Dad didn't even come to my graduation?" Gabriel added softly. "I tried to convince myself that there was something romantic about it. You know: a solitary figure in a black gown, ducking around all the happy families, a musician, forsaken by his own flesh and blood . . ."

Emma slipped her fingers into mine. "So what happened after that?" she asked.

"I better let Sarah tell it," Gabriel mumbled. "I need a drink first." He disappeared around the corner into the little kitchen nook.

"Are you toasting Raj Bhutto?" I called after him, trying to lighten the mood.

He laughed. "Is that some sort of subtle attempt at an

apology? For reading something you shouldn't have?"

I had to smile, too. "So you knew about that, huh?" I asked.

"Of course." The refrigerator door opened and closed. Ice cubes clinked in a glass. Gabriel reappeared with a tumbler of brown liquor, heavy on the liquor.

"I read it, too," Emma confessed. "Do you want it back? It's in Hen's room."

"Nah, keep it," Gabriel said. He took a sip.

"Keep what?" Sarah asked.

"My memoir," Gabriel said, gesturing to the pile of manuscripts. He shot me a quick glance. He probably knew what I was thinking: *A very long love letter to my sister.*

"Tell the rest of the story, Sarah," Emma prompted.

Sarah took a deep breath. "Right. So anyway, after we heard that Gabriel's father was cutting him off, we—"

"Who's we?" Emma interrupted.

"Our circle of friends," Sarah said. "Me; my best friend, Madeline; and the guys in Gabriel's band, Rich and Tony. We just couldn't believe that Mr. Stern could be so *evil*. But he was. And the way it happened . . ." She shook her head and laughed. "I still can't believe it myself."

"What?" I practically screamed, about to jump out of my skin. "Tell us already!"

"I tagged along with Gabriel when he went to make stickers to promote a gig that Friends was playing near campus," she explained. "It was the last gig they ever played. The stickers were originally supposed to feature the band motto, you know, 'Friend is not a verb.' But at the last second, when we were at Kinko's, I convinced him to change it. I said we should turn the stickers into a big screw-you to his dad. Something that would scare him—a warning, almost, that Gabriel wasn't alone, that his friends were his family, and we would all figure out a way to get back at his dad. So Gabriel printed up five hundred that said Steal Your Parents' Money instead." She chuckled. "Ring any bells?"

Holy crap.

Emma dropped my hand. Our eyes bulged. We both started cracking up.

"You?" Emma shouted at my sister. "You're the unsung mystery genius behind Steal Your Parents' Money?"

Sarah looked embarrassed. "If you want to call me that . . ."

"That's exactly what you are," Gabriel said. "The unsung mystery genius."

"Please, Gabriel," she muttered.

He turned to us. "See, none of us had any idea that the stickers would be the next big thing. Blogged about and twittered about . . . they were actually on the *news*."

I nodded. I remembered. How could I forget?

"We all got a kick out of how different people tried to take credit for it," Sarah added. "And that's when it started. We were all in on this delicious little secret, the five of us. It just sort of snowballed from there. We convinced ourselves that we'd founded some kind of revolutionary underground movement.

We decided we *should* steal our parents' money. Starting with Gabriel's dad. Why not? He was the living embodiment of all those Wall Street swindlers who sunk the economy and walked away with a fortune. It wasn't revenge; it was a public service. We'd only take a few million. That was a drop in the bucket to him. And then we'd all disappear somewhere and live happily ever after."

"And that's exactly what happened," Gabriel finished. "Well, not the happily ever after part. The snowball turned into an avalanche. And it swept us all down with it. We robbed my dad of about two million dollars and split to the Dominican Republic. But the thing is . . ."

"There is no happily ever after," Sarah finished.

I shook my head, still staring at Emma. "I can't believe it."

"I know." Gabriel took another sip from his glass. "And I swear to you, Hen, I'm still asking myself: When and how and why did we reach that point? *That's* the question. I don't believe in accidents, but there's no denying the *randomness* of it all. Suddenly we were trapped in a huge house we could never leave—"

"No, no, no," Sarah interrupted. "There was nothing random about it. We were totally united up until the day we got there."

Gabriel tilted his head. "Were we?" he asked in a melancholy voice. "I don't know. I always felt like we were less of a pack and more of a giant spiderweb. Our group friendship started with the bond between you and me, and then it exploded into a sticky mess. But what *is* friendship, anyway? It's just a big tangled jumble of shared experiences. 'I did X, Y, and Z with these people, so they must be my friends.'"

Sarah shook her head. "That's a cop-out. You and I were closer than that."

Gabriel stared down at his drink.

The silence in the room thickened.

"You know, there's something I never told you, Gabriel," Sarah said, suddenly sounding urgent. "And I guess I'm going to have to say this in front of my little brother and his best friend, which is fine, but . . ." She held her breath. "Okay. Gabriel, the main reason—above all others—why I did any of this was to impress *you.*"

Gabriel nearly dropped his glass. The ice cubes rattled. "Excuse me?"

Sarah nodded. "It's true. I never realized how jealous I was of Madeline, of how you had a crush on her. And when we came up with the big plan to rip off your dad . . . I wanted to show you that I was just as crazy and smart and out there as *she* is."

"But that's just wrong," Gabriel protested.

"So what? You know what else? I also thought that it would turn out to be a *joke.* I mean we've always been so detached and ironic with one another—all five of us. We've always had these walls built around ourselves. Just listen to the way we *talk.*"

Gabriel shook his head. "But what about that stuff you said about *your* parents? That you weren't just doing it because of *my* dad. That you did it because they drive you crazy?"

Sarah lifted her shoulders. "They do drive me crazy, but that was a cop-out, too." All at once she turned to me. "Hen, you know the only reason they've been obsessed with your finding a job this summer is because they're terrified that you'll turn out like me. That you'll turn out to be a criminal. That's why they didn't tell you what happened. They *knew*. Gabriel's dad called them and told them that he was out two million dollars and that he had a hunch who took it. But Mom and Dad didn't want the police to find us, so they kept it a secret."

I had no idea what to say. I didn't even know how I *felt*.

"I'll make sure he doesn't turn into a criminal, Sarah," Emma said quietly. "I'll keep him on a tight leash."

Sarah smiled softly. "Thanks." She turned back to Gabriel. "But, look. The thing is, I did it to prove to them what I wanted to prove to you as well . . . that I wasn't just a good girl. That I could be bad."

"But why would you want to prove that?" Gabriel said, stepping toward her. "It doesn't make any sense. You *are* good—"

"Ahem!" Emma cleared her throat. "Just a guess here. But maybe also part of the reason Sarah did it was because her parents are so *overprotective*, and part of the reason you did it is because your dad isn't protective *at all*? I mean, I'm saying this as the only relatively sane human being in this room—emphasis on 'relatively'—and, ah, also because my own insane parents fall somewhere in the middle."

Gabriel chewed his lip, nodding thoughtfully. "I don't know. You may be right."

Sarah tossed her hat on his unmade futon. "So, look. I sold the house to Karl. I've got a cashier's check from Banco Federal in my suitcase for almost three million dollars, made out to Roger Stern. It's all over now. All of it. No more house, no more crime, no more stolen money. Do you forgive me?"

"What the hell are you talking about?" Gabriel shouted. "I should be asking *you* that. That's why I made you come back to the States with me! I was supposed to figure this part out myself! And now you've gone and made everything right on your own? Jesus, Sarah!" He slammed the drink down on top of the pile of manuscripts, spilling some of the liquor. "What's your problem? *I* was supposed to fix this. Not you! You're always fixing everything for me!"

I still have absolutely no idea why, but this compelled Sarah to pounce on Gabriel and start kissing him. *Blecch.* I suppose I should have foreseen a sappy make-out moment. I mean, I *got* it now. Gabriel knew so much about Emma and me because he lived a mirror image. But I hadn't imagined his epiphany moment with my sister would be so in-your-face. It was almost grotesque.

"I think we're embarrassing Hen and Emma," Gabriel whispered, pulling away.

"I don't care," she said, clinging to him. "Gabriel, remember that book I got you in Puerto Plata, the one on that indigenous Caribbean tribe, the Tainos?"

Gabriel swallowed. "Of course."

"Remember how the names the Tainos gave each other were so beautiful? They all spoke to the person's identity. The one who heals. The one who sows. The one who battles. If you had a Taino name, you know what it would be?" She leaned forward and whispered something in his ear. His face turned bright red.

Now I *really* wanted to gag. Note to self: Never be as insane, secretive, and pretentious as my sister or her friends. Never allow things to get to the point where robbing Emma's father would seem like the only solution to some invented problem. On the other hand, never be as detached or ironic, either— Jesus, listen to me. I sound like Gabriel freaking—

The intercom rang: *BZZZT!*

Everybody winced. Our eyes all flew to Gabriel.

"I bet that's Madeline and Karl," Sarah said. Her voice shook slightly. "I told them to meet us here."

I turned to Emma. I wondered if she was thinking the same thing I was—that to cap off all this insanity, we were about to meet a real-live, eighty-year-old Nazi. It was kind of fitting, in its own fantastical way.

"Well, there's only one way to find out," Gabriel said. He stepped over to the door and pressed the button. "Hello?"

"It's your father, Gabriel," a tinny voice barked through the static. "I've brought the police."

Uh-oh. A Nazi might have been preferable.

Emma's grip tightened around my fingers, cutting off the circulation.

"And Sarah Birnbaum's parents, too!" my mother's distorted voice cried. "Where the hell are my children?"

My face twisted. *Jesus.*

Emma giggled. Sarah shook her head, stricken.

Gabriel, on the other hand, remained calm. "So here it goes. Time to ante up."

"What do you think will happen?" Sarah asked fearfully.

"I'm not sure," he said, pressing down on the button to let them in. "But whatever happens, it'll be the right thing. Even if I have to go to jail . . . or whatever. But hopefully, my dad will just take the check and let me off the hook." He grinned. "You know, Sarah, I've always wanted to introduce my dad to your parents."

A tear fell from Sarah's cheek. "Please don't joke around right now," she said.

"It's not a neat ending, is it?" I whispered as Gabriel opened the door.

He glanced at me with a puzzled smile. "What do you mean, Hen?"

My heart pounded. Footsteps approached. "It's not a neat ending to your memoir. You said you had to find an ending."

"Oh, no." He laughed. "Don't worry, Hen. This isn't the ending. How could it be? It's kind of a screwy story, you know? It's just what happens next. The story never ends. Not until we all kick the bucket."

EPILOGUE
Why the Band Journey Sucks, and What This Says About Life

Gabriel's evil dad decided not to press charges, thank God. He seemed very happy with the three-million-dollar check Sarah handed him.

So it *was* sort of a neat ending—at least on that front.

Not long after he and the cops and my parents burst in, Emma and I decided to slip out. Gabriel's East Village crash pad was just a little too crowded with crazy people. Besides, we needed to psych ourselves up for Journey. My first concert ever at Madison Square Garden! With the most heinous possible band! (Okay, okay. Styx would have been more heinous.) My parents let me go without a fight. Honestly, they were still too pissed at Sarah for disappearing again. They were still yelling at her when we left.

About the concert . . .

As I later found out, Journey performed with a substitute singer. A *permanent* substitute singer. That's right: The earnest cheeseball who fronted the band that night was not the same male diva who gave the world such hits as "Lovin', Touchin', Squeezin'," "Don't Stop Believin'," and "Any Way You Want It."

I thought to myself, then why are all these retirement-age people showing him the love? Don't they see that Journey took the easy way out? Instead of calling it quits like they should have, they hit the road with a fraud. They *cheated* their loyal fans.

See, if I learned anything from Sarah and Gabriel that day, it's that there *is* no easy way out. Of anything. You can pretend like something is perfect—a crime, a friendship that should be something more, a washed-up band with a fake singer—but sooner or later, the Unseen Hand will come knocking at your door.

But maybe I'm overthinking things. I've been doing that a lot lately (Gabriel's fault). There's probably no connection at all between Journey and a valuable life lesson. Of course there isn't. Jesus.

Honestly, as far as the Unseen Hand goes, it should have wrung that guy's neck. The Journey front man, I mean. It was a terrible, terrible show. I've never seen anything more horrendous, not even on VH1 Classic. And in real life there's no way to change the channel.

But, hey, the fans seemed to enjoy it. Fat bald men and gray-haired women even raised their lighters at one point. (I think the song that prompted the flood of emotion was, in fact, called "Lights." They're not big on subtlety, Journey.) Mr. Wood shouted "Disco sucks!" five separate times during this number, one for each beer he drank.

Emma owes me one.

Then again, I owe her one, too. I mean, who knows what would have happened if she hadn't showed up at my door that morning and kissed me? I might have even given up my fantasy of being a rock star. That is, instead of bugging Mr. Wood all night to agree to listen to our demo until he finally broke down and said, "Fine, goddammit, now shut your pie hole!"

APPENDIX

The Document I Received in an Email Attachment a
Week Later

The Heist

By Gabriel Stern

Contact number: 347 555 7809

Email: gsternfugitive@webmail.com

Intro: A Surprisingly Lame Thing to Say

My father's all-time favorite cliché is: "Be careful what you wish for, or it might come true." He uses it as often as he can (or at least he did back when I was still in touch with him)—when I applied to Columbia, for instance. He'd also said it to my mother when she was still alive, when she told me she wished I would grow up. I never understood why he liked it so much. It's a surprisingly lame thing to say, even for him.

Phase One

Sarah told me that robbing my father of almost two million dollars would make me feel "tingly"—like the way you feel when you're about to hook up with someone for the first time. But this is the way I feel when I'm about to pee in my pants. There's nothing "tingly" about it. Maybe we should wait. It's the middle of summer. It's too hot to think straight. We could put it off until Labor Day, until after we move out of the loft. The money will still be there.

7:03 P.M.

"It's almost time," I announce.

The five of us pace the living room. We avoid one another's eyes.

My T-shirt is soaked with sweat. The air conditioner is broken. We leave a hastily scrawled apology for the owners of our illegal sublet, along with five hundred dollars to buy a new unit. The humidity is stifling. The air in Chinatown is cream-of-homeless soup, uncollected garbage consommé. I'll have to wash myself down with a prison hose when this is all over. . . .

No, no: Bad idea to think about prison.

"Hey, Mad? Don't you think you should get going?"

"Relax, Gabriel. The reservation is at eight."

Madeline has never looked more beautiful. She's Renée Zellweger in Jerry Maguire, *decked out in jewelry and evening wear: an exquisite actress, utterly charming.*

"Do they serve vegetarian dishes at this place?" *Sarah asks.* "I'd like to eat a vegetarian dish in honor of Hen. Seeing as I'm never going to see him again."

"It's a steak house," *Rich points out.*

I'm barely listening. Even after all these years, I still can't believe that my dad actually dines at Sparks Steak House. It's almost too fitting. It's ludicrous. There's a legacy of foul deeds associated with the place. Mafiosi used to eat there all the time. John Gotti had Paul Castellano rubbed out in front of Sparks. My dad is just as fat and slick and corrupt as both of them. Maybe even more so.

"I bet they serve big salads," *Tony says.*

Sarah shrugs. "As long as I get a good meal. I'm hungry." *She is wearing makeup: eyeliner, blush, and lipstick. She never wears makeup. It makes her look clownish and sleazy, like a prostitute. Some men might find it sexy. Older men.*

Phase Two

We're committed. Sarah and Madeline are already on their way to Sparks. Rich and Tony are on their way to my Madison Avenue apartment. My home. Where I spent senior year, alone. Dad and me and ten big rooms.

I gave them the key to the back staircase. Once inside, they will slink into my dad's study, where Tony will to proceed to hack into the fat pig's bank accounts on his own computer. STEAL YOUR PARENTS' MONEY.

None of us have any concerns about Tony's capabilities. Only three days ago, he hacked into the New York City mayor's office, just to show off. He's more gung ho about this than any of us, even me. He sees it as an intellectual challenge, devoid of any moral implications, like doing the crossword puzzle. Or at least that's the impression he gives us.

I consider jumping into a cab and chasing them. But I know it's too late. In essence, we were committed to The Plan yesterday. We were committed the moment Madeline called Dad and suggested that they meet to talk about my future.

Dad goes to Sparks tonight believing that Madeline is trying to help mend his relationship with me.

Dad has always loved Madeline. On several occasions, he told me that Madeline is too good for me, and that I'll never hook up with her. He thinks that I need to learn some humility.

On the phone, Madeline told him that it breaks her heart to see me cut off from my own flesh and blood. Maybe she can help Dad reach some sort of understanding . . . if he's willing to listen.

"Oh, by the way, can Sarah join us? Did Gabriel ever mention to you that Sarah has a thing for older men? Her last boyfriend was a fifty-year-old investment banker. Just like you, Mr. Stern."

I picture the dinner as Madeline says it will unfold.

Cocktails first, courtesy of Dad. Lots of witty banter and laughs. They settle into their meals. They get comfortable with one another. Dad notices Sarah stealing glances at him. He never paid any attention whenever I introduced them, but thanks to Madeline he suddenly sees that this girl is very attractive. She's twenty-two—but hey, he messed around with one of his secretaries, and she was twenty-six! What difference does four years make? The girl is still legal, right? Barely, sure—but as a veteran of countless lawsuits, Dad appreciates the difference.

Sarah is starting to get a little tipsy.

They're all starting to get tipsy.

Madeline finally broaches the subject of my future. She asks Roger (it's all right if she calls him Roger, isn't it?) to step back and think of me as a helpless little boy. No, don't think of him as an adult. Think of him as your son. Your baby. Just look at a picture of him. You have a picture, don't you?

Yes, he does. In his wallet.

Oh, goody! Madeline wants to see it.

He hands it over, nearly shoving it into her dress.

Under the table, Sarah starts to fondle his knee. Now we're talking. Things are looking good. Madeline is staring at the photo. It's Dad's chance to play Casanova. He turns to Sarah—

Madeline pockets his bankcard. She returns the wallet and excuses herself to go to the bathroom.

9:37 p.m.

I arrive at the corner of Forty-sixth Street and Third Avenue. I'm secretly hoping that Madeline won't show. I imagine that something went wrong: that Sarah decided to forgo the salad and ate a huge steak and barfed, that Dad stormed out of the restaurant . . . that Madeline never got the card. I imagine that The Plan failed completely.

But my dad is too predictable, too lecherous. Madeline appears within seconds.

I can't stand still. The streetlights are very bright. I feel we should be meeting in the dark, even though I know we're safe. We're anonymous: two pedestrians in the chaos of midtown. But I can't keep my eyes from darting at all of the passersby.

"Relax, Gabriel," she says. "He thinks I'm in the bathroom, remember? Girls take a long time in the bathroom."

She hands me the card. It's gold. I can tell by her smile that she appreciates the symbolism. Gold: the color of buried treasure.

For a moment, I stare at it. The printed matter is in Dutch, except for his name and a Visa logo. This is real. This is actually happening. I can feel my heart against my rib cage—a convict's fists, banging against jailhouse bars.

"Any problems?" I whisper. My voice quavers.

"No," she says. She is perfectly calm.

"How's Sarah holding up?"

"She deserves an Oscar for tonight. We owe her, Gabriel. I wish you could see her. That fat slimeball . . ." She doesn't finish. "Sorry. I know he's your dad."

She kisses me—very quickly—and disappears back down the block.

Phase Three

I've finally done it.

I've kissed Madeline. I've made contact.

After that, my perspective on the evening changes. I'm ready to kick ass. True, the kiss was brief, but it was a historic moment, a harbinger of the thrills to come in our brand-new mansion on the ocean. By this time tomorrow, I'll be dancing naked in the sand with her. And more.

My perspective on our entire group's dynamic changes, too. We're no longer merely five losers who share a love of the nineties. No . . . we're a real band now. More than Friends. Even though Sarah and Madeline don't play instruments, they're in, too. In fact, I see the five of us now as avatars of Fleetwood Mac.

I'm Mick Fleetwood—the outsider in some ways, yet the glue that holds the band together. Rich and Madeline are Lindsey Buckingham and Stevie Nicks, respectively. They're the creative force, the shining stars . . . the lovers who create the music. Tony is John McVie, the utility man (all right, the nerd). And Sarah is Christine McVie: the funny, sensitive iconoclast who blossoms into a dignified beauty. The one Mick Fleetwood should have hooked up with.

The only difference between Fleetwood Mac and us is that Sarah and Tony were never married. Also, I'm a lot shorter than Mick Fleetwood.

But the vital similarities remain. The connections are undeniable. The Plan is our masterpiece: both our *Rumours* and our reunion tour. It's a sign. I would never have watched *Behind the Music: Fleetwood Mac* if it weren't. As Lindsey and Stevie, Rich and Madeline must break up. As Mick, I must have a torrid romance with Rich's soon-to-be former girlfriend.

And then, in a bizarre twist, I will also hook up with Christine McVie: my best friend.

There is no other possible sequence of events.

10:35 p.m.
Tony's call comes.
"Hello?"
"You get the card?"
"Yup." My heart is thumping again. I glance around the banking center on East Fifty-first Street: the rows of ATMs, the grubby tile floor littered with receipts, the harsh fluorescent lights. I am alone. It occurs to me that this is the very first time I've ever bought a cell phone with my own money (as opposed to Dad's money). It might be Tony's first time, too. Two cell phones for a single call: this call. $103.97 split five ways. It represents the only money we spent on The Plan, aside from cab fare and the money to replace the air conditioner.

"I'm putting the card in now," I announce. I picture Tony and

Rich on the other end, sitting in my dad's darkened study, their faces lit by the bluish glow of the computer. "It says touch here to proceed in English . . ."

The image of a keypad appears on the screen, along with the words: PLEASE ENTER YOUR PERSONAL IDENTIFICATION NUMBER.

"The code is one zero eight four nine three," Tony says.

Pulsating blood fills my ears. I can barely hear him. I press the numbers. My fingers leave moist traces on the glass.

PLEASE WAIT A MOMENT WHILE WE PROCESS YOUR INFORMA-TION . . .

"Now it's asking me what kind of transaction I want to make," I whisper.

"Withdrawal from savings. It should give you a list of six different accounts."

Presto: Six rectangles flash on the screen: one on top of the other, each filled with a string of digits. I know a hidden video camera must be taping me right now. I force the thought from my mind. We'll be long gone before anybody sees the footage.

"Select the top one," Tony instructs. "It should start with three two eight."

I obey. Dollar amounts appear, ranging from $20 to $1500.

"How much should I take out?" I ask. My voice is thick and shaky, unrecognizable to myself.

"Fifteen hundred from each account," Tony says. I can tell from a change in tone that he's smiling now. "We're flying first-class tomorrow morning. I want to do some duty-free shopping."

The machine whirs and hums.

The slot opens.

A crisp pile of bills emerges, like a baby from the womb.

I smile, too, even though I am nauseated. We are committed. The paper feels cool against my hot fingers. I'm tempted to rub it against my forehead. I fight back sickness. I force the righteous venom to course through my veins. My father deserves this. It's not an impulse that went awry, a whim that snowballed into an atrocity. It's justice. Divine justice. Like the writing on the wall in the book of Daniel: MENE, MENE, TEKEL, UPHARSHIN . . .

"Got it?" Tony asks.

"Got it," I say.

He laughs. "We did it, then, didn't we?"

"We did it."